The
Immortals
Prison Hearts

ISBN: 978-1-387-17758-5

Acknowledgements

I want to thank all my family for the support they gave me while I sorted myself out to write this book.

To my mammabear who is always there for me, and to my Dad who begrudgingly drove me places due to my lack of transport.

I want to thank all my friends and supporters that bought art from me to keep me fed.

And Finally to my Dog Houdini.

My pupper is the light and bane of my life, he has kept me sane, he is also the reason why I got overly distracted and procrastinated!

And Thank you everyone reading this, as it means you bought my book, you beautiful wonderful person you!

There is more to life than

What we know or what we see.

All we have to do is open our eyes

And really look to see

What is in front of us.

The Immortals

Prison

Hearts

By L. Scanlon

Chapter One

The girl who started it all

Opening the door to a new class can be rather nerve racking, but to Crystal it was nothing new, her parents had died just over eight years prior to this day, and in that time she had been placed in nine different schools, yet every time she never seemed to settle, this one was her last option, well unless her guardian decided to move that was.

As she walked into the class room as her name was being written upon the board, she focused on the squeaking of the marker as it spelled out her name, it was better than paying attention to the voices of interested students that began to blur into a flurry of whispers. She turned to face what would be her new 'friends' with an uninterested expression as her homeroom teacher began the introductions

"Quiet down now, Class this is Crystal Heath, Say hello to everyone Crystal" She looked to the teacher briefly before returning her dark gaze to the class, nineteen eyes looked to her, some filled with curiosity some with disinterest.

One pair of dark eyes seemed to mirror her own and she decided to focus on them "My name is Crystal, nice to meet you" this seemed to please the teacher as she continued the introduction in the usual fashion which caused her to shake her head a small bit "Crystal, will be joining us this term, please make her feel welcome.

Crystal, if you could take a seat at the back, next to..." the teacher began to look at his list for the boys name, there were two seats at the back, one next to the window, beside a sullen blond, and the other was next to the student with the dark eyes she had been staring at.

"Peter Faben"

The blond boy looked up to the teacher from what he had been doing, he seemed a bit startled by his name being called as though he was only now aware of something happening, and to Crystal's surprise the most amazing pair of eyes turned to look at her. They were green, but not the typical big green eyes you see everywhere.

His eyes seemed to have some kind of light trapped within them, they were like nothing she had ever seen before, yet as quickly as their gaze met it also broke, as Peter went right back to working on whatever he had been doing before his name was called.

Crystal could hardly bring herself to move after that, but she forced her feet to move and tried to hide the shocked expression from her face, the whispers returned as pulled the chair out from the desk.

She caught a few of them, silly things like, what was her age and if she was single, and she sat back trying to ignore them, she knew full well that she was seen as good looking, but the was not full of herself or conceited about it, if anything it annoyed her that people only paid interest in her for how she looked, she had pale skin and dark brown hair, her features were slight, not what you would called curvy, but not so much that you would mistake her for a boy, her eyes were a true black, and it was thanks to a recent surge of 'vampire' popularity, that she became more desirable, for her that it didn't seem all that important, she just found it irritating.

When she took her seat, the boy beside her seemed to almost lean away, and even though it was subtle, she still noticed, yet she wasn't given time to think upon it too much as a bleach blond girl sitting in front turned to greet her.

"My name is Sharon, I am vice president of the class, Thomas; The boy over there" at this point Sharon pointed out the guy with the dark eyes she had been staring at first "is the president, if you have any questions you should ask one of us"

9

She was about to thank her for the offer until she was motioned to lean in closer, only once she was close enough, did Sharron lower her voice and continue speaking, but as far as she was concerned, it was not quiet enough to be truly decent for what she had to say.

"I would avoid talking to Peter if I were you, he might look okay but he's a weirdo"

Peter shifted in his seat and obviously pretended not to hear anything, But Crystal's face darkened slightly, "Thank you ... Sharon was it? But I try to make my own judgments on people" With that said she then turned to the blond sitting beside her and extended a hand "My name is Crystal, it is nice to make your acquaintance Peter."

Once again dazzling emerald eyes rose, this time to look to her dark ones, it took a moment, but Peter eventually took her hand and weakly shook it, "Urm... hallo" his voice was quiet, but it held a certain tone to it that almost drew her in, but that was all Peter said to her before looking back to his work, and a few moments after the class started, and that was Crystal's first encounter with the boy who would change her entire world.

--

She was not entirely sure why she wanted to know Peter better, his attitude was cold towards everyone, in the few times she had tried to speak to him he had brushed her off or simply walked away, perhaps Sharon was right? Maybe there was something wrong with him, regardless though, she wanted to get to know him better as there was just something about how he carried himself that made her want to help him, it was odd.

A week passed, all she had gotten from Peter was an occasional Hallo or an odd glance, before she would be dragged away by another student, it seemed that Crystal was rather popular in the school as people with eyes as dark as her seemed to be rare.

Thomas Fletcher, the Class president, was another with similar features, though it seemed that they would not get along well, each time she attempted to talk to him, she would be met with a short reply, or a look of irritation.

Sharon also did not seem very taken with her after the first encounter, though a tall dark haired senior by the name of Victor was making sure Crystal knew he was interested, she was not all that bothered by it really, he was popular, good looking, he was part of the swimming team, meaning he was fit, he had dark brown hair with an odd white patch on the right of his temple, and eyes such a light hazel brown you would think them gold, but as if all that was not good enough,

He was also smart, though why he was chasing her was a mystery.

His first attempt to talk to her resulted in her laughing at him and telling him to try a different bimbo as he seemed to have many to choose from, the second was her calling him a pompous git who only cared about looks.

But the third one was her apologizing to him as she had realized that she had been so rude and they had actually talked, turned out that he was quiet lovely and had taken a shine to her as he had heard that she stood up to Sharon.

In fact her antics on the first day had made quiet the stir and he found her bravery in the face of bullying to be rather endearing, and so it played out that a mere two hours after the announcement of the School dance, that Crystal found herself now with a date and an ultimatum.

You see, as it turned out though, Victor had a fan-club, and said club; after finding out she was asked to go with him, threatened that she had better not get any fancy idea's and an order that she had BETTER be as good a dancer as he was because no one was to make their Victor look bad!

Crystal swore she was a good dancer and that she would not let them down, no matter how strange it was to be in the situation in the first place.

After that the group told her that she could join their club once the dance was over and she proved herself to be worthy of a place.

Now honestly she didn't really care about it, she didn't even know Victor all that well, she only said yes to him because he had in truth been rather nice to her since she had joined the school, the main problem was... She couldn't dance at all, when she had tried to, it could only be described as a tube man in a hurricane.

She knew that she would need to figure something out, but what? A few hours after the whole debacle, she found herself sitting in her class room alone, she was trying to figure out a way to tell Victor that she couldn't go without upsetting him or making him think she didn't like him (she was undecided on that point), but still remain alive afterwards for risk of garnering his fan clubs wrath, after all if dancing badly with him was bad, turning him down would be even worse right?

It was during her contemplations that the door slid open, she looked up to find shocked green eyes staring at her.

"What are you doing here?" Peter said in a hushed tone.

He seemed almost offended by the fact that she was in the room, he literally skulked towards his desk and muttered "you should be out for lunch, like the rest of them"

She got the feeling that to him, it was almost as though her presence was a burden, frowning she looked at him for a moment, sure he was being rude, but there it was again, that want to get to know him, to make his misery melt away

"Why do they treat you that way Peter?" The blond slide back his chair abruptly and made to walk away without a word. She stood with a sense of strange urgency to make him stop, she had to say something, anything to make him stay. "Wait!" She said with a hint of desperation, and he blond halted, but didn't turn around, yet it was enough.

"Sorry I didn't mean, well, I just wanted to know... urm, do you know how to dance?"

This seemed to get the blonds attention, as he turned to once again look at her but still he didn't say anything, he only listened as she spoke, though even she was not sure why she was saying this, but the subject had halted him so she kept with it.

"I need to learn how to dance in three weeks, if I don't I think Victors fan-club might kill me, please, can you help me?"

That was the first time Crystal saw him smile, it was as though someone had turned a light on in the room that she hadn't known was off, and the smile then turned into a laugh, it was a sweet musical laugh, and soon she was laughing with him not really understanding why.

--

After a short talk in the class room Crystal found out that Peter was actually a rather good dancer, he also explained the way the end of year dance worked, apparently there would be a theme to the ball and an organized dance, it was on that dance that people would cast votes, for the last three years Victors club had done all they could to try and make sure he won, though it had not worked last year. Between bullying his dates and making sure they were up to standard, they had become a force to be reckoned with.

Though Victor was apparently unaware of any of this, and was not sure why all the girls he asked out would leave him after a few weeks. Apparently no one was up to the high standards of the club.

Peter joked then about her wanting to fight for Victor at all and she just laughed saying "hey it's not like I have much choice is it? Anyway, should I go back to your house after to practice with you?" this seemed to up him on edge, and all the joy he had been radiating appeared to vanish.

"No, that's not a good idea, My guardian isn't very friendly at the best of times, and I don't think she would like me bringing people home, heh, she doesn't like 'me' going home half the time, I dunno, perhaps none of this is a good idea, after all, I really shouldn't be talking to you"

She frowned again, as she was finding herself doing more and more as it came to people's reactions to Peter "And just why shouldn't you be talking to me? I don't see anything wrong with it?"

Once more the blond seemed to shut down, and she instantly regretted her words. She had to fix this, they had been getting on so well after all

"How about this then, you come to my house, I live with my Aunt, but she doesn't bother me too much, you can show me how to dance there? And if it makes you feel better, I won't talk to you in school, Alright?"

This seemed to work as he nodded, though he still seemed none to pleased about the situation, but Crystal, well she was thrilled with how it worked out, perhaps she would have to thank the fan-club afterwards for giving her this excuse to talk to him, or perhaps not, maybe they wouldn't be ecstatic about the idea of her 'seeing' another guy, she would tell Victor though, after all, she was… kinda dating him right?

After class she found her would be date to tell him about her lesson plans, Victor just laughed and told her that she didn't need to be a good dancer at all, but he didn't mind her getting lessons, when she told him who she was getting the lessons from however his expression changed.

Though not to the revulsion that most had when talking about Peter, Victor seemed… well intrigued somehow, but he said nothing more on it and just smiled saying he would see her tomorrow.

--

Peter said that they might as well start today seeing as he had nothing planned in the evening, she had agreed to it, but now as she stood in her basement and looked at him, she didn't think she was really prepared, well at least it was not what she had thought it would be.

Sweat was dripping from Crystal's face and her shirt was sticking to her back, and for the fifth time Peter stopped her saying 'no no no, your doing it all wrong, you need to be led by the man, not blindly steer yourself around the room like your swinging a cat"

The man 'leading her was a mop, and the room was her basement, Peter sat on the floor giving directions on how she should hold her partner, how her feet should be moving, but she just didn't seem to be able to take it all in, and so also for the fifth time, Peter stood and took a hold of the mop.

"Like this" He said as he held his hand up, holding the mop as though placing his hand on someone's shoulder and held the mop out from him, then pretending to take an imaginary hand in his with the other hand, Crystal just threw her hands up in the air and let out an agitated scream.

"Argh, I am never going to get this before the dance!" She began to march to the door, but a hand upon her own stopped her, Peter's hand was warm, and a heat rushed through her to the feel of it.

"Look... How about this, I will lead you... after that, you can try with the mop again okay... I am not... I don't like doing this sort of thing"

Peter spoke in a quiet tone as he said it, as though he was almost afraid to suggest it in the first place. It didn't take a second thought for her to accept these terms though, and she gripped Peter's hand and led him back into the room.

She could almost feel his heart pounding within his chest as he gripped her hand, though she was not sure why this made him so nervous, after all, surely he would have danced with someone else before right? He was looking away as his fingers curled over her back.

She placed her hand on his shoulder like she had been shown, and looked to how Peter was positioned, he was ridged as though he had a pole for a spine, he took three deep breath and without turning to look at her he whispered ' follow my lead'

Feet began to move, and she staggered trying to keep up, Peter was counting out the pace as they danced, one, two, three, one, two, three, and after a few moments it became easier for her to understand, they danced with the rhythm, keeping to a set circle.

Crystal closed her eyes just letting herself be steered by Peter, so she was not ready for the sudden stop.

Legs became entangled and air began to rush past her ears as she went hurtling to the floor below. She felt Peter's hand gripping hers, but it was too late, she was falling fast and she was taking Peter with her now.

She had bumped her head a bit, but nothing too serious, she opened her eyes to look at the ceiling but saw a mess of golden hair instead.

Peter had fallen on top of her, and for a moment she had the thought of this being some cheesy romance novel and hoped he would look down on her and kiss her, which was of course crazy.

She had only met him that day and knew very little about him, but there it was, call it teenage hormones or whatever, but right now she was in a very happy place and did not want to move.

But Peter obviously did, he did a pushup off her and once more she found herself looking into those shocking eyes, but instead of the romantic vision of him kissing her, he instead stood up and looked away.

"I think that's enough for today… I will come by again on the weekend and we can start the next step" And without even an offer to help her up, he left.

--

Crystal kept thinking about him all that night, and through then to the next morning, there was something about the look he got in his eyes that made her want to know more about him.

Later that morning she pulled a girl in his class aside, she was a plain enough blond girl by the name of Amy, she seemed nice enough so she would be a safe one to ask, well that's what he assumed.

"Peter? Well… I don't really know a lot about him, he has been in our class a few years I guess, he was nice enough at the start but he got into a fight with Thomas, he punched him right in the nose! He was suspended for a week, after that any time people tried to talk to him; he would just look away from them or shout at them to go away, he is a bit of a weirdo really, I know you sit beside him and all, but if I were you, I would ignore him"

She only nodded to the girl as she seemed to be telling the truth, but it didn't really tell her much about what was going on, the only information she really got out of it was that Peter got into a fight with Thomas before he started acting 'weird'.

There was only one thing she could do.

Thomas ate lunch in the courtyard, he was usually alone, and today was no exception, Crystal came up behind him and asked in a low voice "Thomas, May I have a word with you?" The class president didn't even look up he just murmured.

"What do you want?" She moved closer to him and spoke clearer. "I want to know what you and Peter fought about when he first joined the school."

She didn't see the movement, but soon found herself pushed back against a wall and a pair of dark eyes glaring at her, she looked up in slight horror as the he almost screamed at her

"Have you been talking to Peter?! What has he been saying to you?!"

Terror flooded through her as she thought he was going to strike her, but after managing to shake her head he moved back from her and ran a hand through his hair as though to try and calm himself.

"You stay away from him, do you hear me! Peter is nothing but trouble to you, you're not to go near him again"

Thomas stalked away after that and Crystal sank to the ground visibly shaken, just what was all that about?

21

She knew nothing more on what she had come to find out, and now she had more questions. Maybe this really was more trouble than it was worth.

Chapter 2

The boy without friends

Dance lessons were not getting any better, Peter had gone over to Crystal's house as promised that weekend, but after what had happened last time he reverted back to the mop and protested against her attempts to draw him to his feet.

He couldn't risk it, she was so nice to him, and he liked her well enough, but when he got close to people, they always got hurt, be it through some other person hurting them, or some kind of accident, he just never had any luck with friends.

That night was not any better, it had been decided that since it had gotten so late Peter would stay the night, he had protested against it of course but Crystal's aunt insisted, she said she would be too worried about him going home alone, this was strange to him, seeing as no one had worried about him in years, not since his parents had disappeared, and of course this train of thought did nothing to improve his mood.

Not that he was rude mind you, he was just quiet. In fact despite all his failings, he was always polite to adults, those his own age rarely deserved respect. Simple as that. He ate dinner in silence and then quietly asked where he would sleep.

"You can sleep in my room, right aunty Claire?" Crystal said this with an innocent smile on her face and her aunt nodded and laughed. But Peter was not so sure about it, not that anything would happen, but Crystal had an annoying habit of wanting to 'talk'

--

It was later that night as he was laying out his sleeping bag when it started, the 'talking'.

"What has gotten into you Peter?"

"......." Peter grunted softly and just unfurled his covers and began to straighten his pillow, he did not want to get into it, he really didn't.

"Why won't you talk to me?" Crystal took the five strides across the room and griped to his arm, forcing him to face him, Peter looked at her with cold green eyes and furrowed his brow

"Like you talked to Thomas?"

She took a step back from him as he said that, raising a hand to cover her gasp, he half smiled and shook his head

"yeah I heard about it, you are being too nosey, you should just forget about trying to get to know me"

"But why-"

"I will show you how to dance, that's all, don't ask too many questions about me, I don't want you getting hurt"

Peter got beneath his covers then and turned away from the dark haired girl once again.

She was left frowning over him, it was clear that she was not going to get any more out of the blond, and so retreated to her own bed.

She must have been frustrated just lying there not say anything, so she had indignantly turned to face him once again

"I am not afraid of Thomas you know, he just, he caught me off guard"

She said this as she sat up, placing her hands over her knees in a relaxed way. "You know... I know kung fu"

Peter stirred and then gave her a side long glace and shook his head. "If you know kung fu, you would be a better dancer, good night Crystal, we can continue in the morning, and then I'll go home"

Perhaps she had hoped that that would work, but he would say nothing more to her, it was too hard for him, it was weird, she felt familiar to him, not as though he knew her before, but almost like they were the same.

He felt as though she could be someone important to him, but he knew that that was nothing but a pipe dream, after all, he was not supposed to get close to others...

--

The next morning he woke up bright and early, he looked over to Crystal who was still sleeping and smiled slightly, at least he would have some peace for a little while.

He wandered downstairs not actually expecting to see anyone, but the noise of a kettle boiling told him that aunt Claire was awake. He pushed the door open and gave her a sheepish smile, she smiled in return and said "You sleep okay Peter?"

He nodded and took a seat at the counter "Yes, though your niece likes to talk" at this the woman seemed shocked "Well this is news to me, in the years I have had her here, she has never made a real friend, much less wanted to get to know them"

Peter frowned and looked back to where he came from. No friends? But that didn't seem right, she was very popular already in school... but even now that he thought on it, other than him and Victor, she didn't talk to anyone.

"Miss Claire-"
"Just Claire is fine sweety"
"Um okay... well, can you tell me about Crystal?

She put two cups on the table with some milk and sugar poured out a pot of tea and then sat across from him before saying anything.

"Well Peter, it's not that complicated of a story, she lost her parents when she was nine, and has secluded herself since, I think you are the first person she has actually reached out too"

This did nothing to clear up why she got attached to him, but he supposed if her aunt didn't understand it, there was nothing more he could do

"Now it's your turn Peter, just how did you learn to be such a good dancer?"

He smiled a bit and poured out a cup of tea for them both "Well, I live with my cousin, she doesn't much like me, so she put me into classes outside school, I have been to so many that I am hardly ever at home, dancing came from acting, and I suppose Gymnastics too."

"Really? I haven't done that since I was a little girl, I could never get the beam though" She laughed as she said this and Peter chuckled too

"Yeah the beam was hard, but it was not as bad as when I had to learn Canoeing, being trapped in a turned over boat is not my idea of fun, but my guardian thought it would teach me... 'A life lesson in survival skills' I think she was secretly hoping I would drown"

'Why would she want you to drown?"

The question came from behind him and he almost choked on his tea from the jump he got, it took him a moment to compose himself before he stood to face the dark haired girl.

"Are you ready, we should start early to get this over with"

That said Peter started for the basement, Leaving Crystal and her aunt looking confused to the sudden coldness, She followed him down the stairs where he was waiting for her mop in hand.

"Okay Crystal, I want you to practice the turns again, but this time hold the mop"

She sprang at him as he said this and covered his mouth before shifting her glance from side to side..

"Peter... I think the mop is trying to kill me... I can't dance with it" She said this whilst glaring at the offending cleaning instrument.

He removed her hand and looked at her with an expression that was a mix of exasperation and amusement.

"I know what you're trying to do Crystal, and it won't work, I am not dancing with you again, last time... it just felt weird."

"Please Peter, I am not learning right this way" She said as she griped to his hands "and if I step on you, you can... you can give me the mop again!"

He frowned and took a deep breath, just like he had before, but unlike the last time, this was in defeat, despite trying to keep her at bay, this girl was just too likable.

"Alright... but you're not holding my hand right, your back needs to be straighter, and your elbow higher, you place your hand on my shoulder lightly, not as stiff as you have been, raise your chin, and hold that form as we are moving"

He barked out the orders without looking at her, he could almost feel the smugness radiating from her, but it was better than her pestering.

"And Don't think this means you have won, I am only doing this to stop you complaining at me, the more you whine at me, the more delayed I am!" Peter said it as he gripped her hand tight. " on three"

It turned out Crystal was just as bad as he remembered, though he supposed it took practice to get it right, but it was not as though they had much time to prepare, three weeks that was it, and even if they spent each weekend dancing throughout, he knew it would not be enough time to learn everything there was to learn, it would be better to just focus on one type of dancing.

Three hours later and she was improving a bit, Claire had brought down her laptop so they could listen to music while dancing and it really helped, though Crystal wanting to listen to more modern music made it pretty weird.

But he eventually convinced her to listen to Chopin. It was all going fine until he reached the end of a set and dipped her a bit too much.

His hand slipped lower on her back and he lent in closer, he could feel his heart hammering in his chest, and he audibly swallowed as he shifted his weight to keep his balance this time.

It felt like hours, just looking into her dark eyes, but there was something else, a light in them, they were calling for him, and that was when another voice entered his mind 'can you feel her power Peter?'

He felt as though all the blood had drained from him, this was not the first time he had heard this voice, but it was the first time it had been so clear and the first time he had been awake for it, he straightened up with her and moved away

"That's enough" He was shaking now and he turned from her. Walking up the stairs he clenched his fist tightly, this was not how he expected the day to end, right now he just wanted to get home.

"I have to go now Crystal. We have one more weekend before the dance, I can't come over during the week... I have things I have to do"

This seemed to snap Crystal out of her daze, she chased after him and gripped to his shirt "Peter, sorry, I did something weird again, but you don't have to go"

He just shrugged away from her and continued up and out through the kitchen, he gave Claire a small wave as he left but was quick about getting out of there, and the last thing he heard was "Did you and your friend have a fight?" before he ran from the house.

--

The road was quiet and the air was calm, it sounded like a Sunday should, and it felt like a Sunday should too, Peter could hear the children that lived beside him playing, and he looked into the yard as he passed.

Upon seeing him they scurried away to hide behind a tree. It wasn't surprising to him and he just ignored it. He was well used to the children reacting that way. It was not really their fault anyway.

He reached up to the lock on his front door, he had to jiggle the key because he knew that the door jammed if he didn't.

31

A musty smell greeted him and he could hear the telly blaring in the sitting room. It had to be his guardian, Megan.

Peter slipped off his jacket and placed his bag to the floor, he peeked into the room to see her sitting there, and he said nothing, he just began to walk as quietly as he could up the stairs, but before he could reach the second step, a voice halted him.

"You didn't come home last night. Where were you, I know you didn't go to the library like you said you were, and I doubt it lets people stay overnight even if you say you did. Were you staying over with a friend from class? I told you about that before, about how you..."

"I wasn't doing anything" Peter interjected "I was walking home, and felt like staying out. That's all. Besides, you made it perfectly clear to me already that I am not allowed to have friends."

"That's right, you're not" The woman said it calmly and then smiled softly placing a hand to Peter's cheek "It's not like you need anyone else is it? Now get cleaned up, you have tai-chi classes in three hours and I am not about to drive you"

Megan rarely went out of the house, all she seemed to do was sit around and boss him about, he was convinced she only looked after him because she got to live off his dowry till he turned eighteen, well only one year to go!

Peter had not always lived like this. He had actually been a rather normal kid a few years ago. He and his parents planned to move to the area barely four years past, he had enrolled into the school and they all seemed set to be happy enough, but on the day they were set to move in.

His parents never arrived to the house. A search was done for them, but they never turned up.

A month later Megan was assigned as his guardian, being his closest relative on his mother's side, she was like a second cousin or something, she was barely six years older than him, but she was still classed as old enough to be a guardian.

She used visit them a lot when he was younger. He had never really liked her back then, and he really disliked her now.

As he closed the door to his room and pulled off his socks, he began to wonder, as he had many times in the last years, what could have happened to his parents?

Nothing was ever found of them, not even the car they had been driving. Peter remembered asking to go in the delivery van. He had been so excited about it. But now... now he just regretted not going with his parents, maybe if he had been there...

A loud banging came to his door "Are you ready yet? If you're late people will start asking questions! If I have another person at this door because of you I swear!"

Peter opened the door and glared at her. "I get it, I'm going" with nothing to eat he left the house, he didn't even have time to change, but he took fresh clothing with him.

Peter knew what most people thought of him, he even had a feeling Megan believed it. People were blaming his parent's disappearance on him, saying he had had problems as a child, that's why they moved away.

So Peter had to behave. He had to stay quiet, and he had to make sure not to draw attention on himself. Megan reminded him of that almost every day.

He forced his arms back through the sleeves of his coat and closed the door with a soft click. He had three classes to go to today, first was tai-chi, then he had archery two hours after that, and finally he had gymnastics.

He began the walk to town and took a deep breath. If Megan found out he was staying over at Crystal's house, he wasn't sure what she would do, so he decided to keep it a secret, that way, no one would get hurt.

Chapter 3

A Plan Set in Motion

'Alright class settle down"

The teacher at the front of class spoke to them without much muster, he seemed to have no real energy about him at all, earning him the name professor sloth, though his actual name was Karl Smith.

The room was buzzing and no one seemed to notice him as he strode to the center of the noise with a pair of dusters in his hands.

One powered class later and silence had descended, giving the now smug looking teacher its full attention

'Now class, we have to decide on a theme for the spring dance, as you all know, it falls onto our heads if anything goes wrong for the seniors, we need to make this as special a time for them as we possibly can, as it will be the last year they will spend in this school and we need to make it a memorable."

It would have been a nice sentiment if he sounded like he meant any of it. "Anyone with valid ideas please raise your hands. No Simon, we are not having a swimwear theme"

An energetic youth with pale skin, gray-blue eyes and black shaggy hair that had waved his hand in the air put it back to the table with a distinct pout and a few of the girls giggled.

That left three hands raised, Sharon, A tall brown haired fellow by the name of John, and Peter.

The teacher Stared at Peter's hand for a while, before looking to Sharon and pointing to her first.

"I propose we have a Hawaiian setting, we could spend the rest of the week making leis and our refreshments could be exotic fruits"

"YEAH! And coconut shell bikinis!"

"No Simon" Sharon interjected "The outfits do not only consist of what they show on television"

" Is that your full suggestion" The sullen teacher asked while giving her a look that told her he didn't really care what they did as long as something was decided so he could go back to reading his book and letting the class teach itself.

Sharon nodded and he pointed at Peter.

"Alright broody boy" The class left out a giggle but fell silent as a duster was once more raised "Let's hear your idea so the class can reject it and go with Sharon's"

Peter's chair screeched as he stood, he was never one for making announcements, but something stuck in his head and it wanted out, also he had another reason for it, he let his gaze fall on Crystal, if only for a moment before he looked into the deadened eyes of his teacher

"My idea Me Smith..." Peter shuffled and took a deep breath, they had seen him do it before, and it clicked with Crystal that Peter did this to find some courage

"Why not have the dance set in a Victorian style? The girls would get to wear big Victorian dresses, and the guys would wear tail coat suits, we could learn dances and, well, there are lots of foods that could be used for the refreshments... and it's kinda cold around our spring... so, with the outfits... well... it was just an idea"

Peter's words trailed away at the end and he sat back down and withdrew into himself, the truth was, if they did anything else, she wouldn't know the right dances, What Peter didn't realize was most of the class was staring at him.

John then stood and recited his idea, he suggested futuristic with leather suits and Jedi outfits, this also went down well with Simon, who was told he was a duster away from detention.

"Alright class" The apathetic teacher leant to his desk and gazed over the class "We can go with Sharon's idea of flouncing around in grassy skirts while drinking out of pineapples, broody boy's idea of fancy dress and fairytale dances, or not clever enough to put some thought into it boys star-wars and bondage theme, we vote now"

All the class could vote, except those that gave ideas

"Sharon's"

Five people raised their hands to that

"Peter's"

Twelve people's hands rose to the air

"And finally John's"

One hand rose, and it belonged to Simon, who slowly put it down again.

"Alright, now that we have that out of the way, Sharon, I am sure you will veto being in the class committee so I suppose you should start working on your leis class"

Sharon stood up, looked to Peter, and then to Thomas who had been staring at her.

"I actually like Peter's idea more Mr Smith"

--

After break was English, the class had been a buzz with ideas on what they would be wearing and where they would get there outfits from, half of the fun of it, was the short notice, it made it harder for the well-off people to have things specially made for them, so everyone had an equal chance.

Peter had his book open and was scanning a page when a note was passed to him, he looked at it for a moment and then looked around to see if anyone was looking at him

"Thank you"

That was all the note said, but Peter shook his head and scribbled a reply

"You're not meant to be talking to me in school, that was the deal"

He put it to the pasty girls table and got one sent back almost right away

"I'm not, I am writing to you, there is a difference"

Peter could not help the smile that came over him and set to writing once more

"Now you're just being picky"

"Well I am right, so I am not breaking any agreement"

"I will send you to the janitor's closet to study if you're not careful"

"I would not mind getting some studying done after school"

It was as Peter opened the last note that a loud cough from the front of the class set him Jumping

"Read it out Peter"

His eyes shot around the room, this was the second time he had to stand in front of people and he went visibly red this time.

"It says... I... would not mind getting some Studying done after school..."

The Woman huffed and strode up to his seat and stared at the paper, then she stared at him, then to the paper again...

"Well, I can't really give out to you for that, but, No more notes in my class, that applies to you also Crystal"

Peter grinned and the change in his features was astounding, it was enough to get more than a few of the girls staring at him, Crystal's head was down, but her shoulders were shaking, and Peter punched her on her arm, hard enough to have Crystal clinging to it mouthing 'ow'

Peter spent the rest of the class trying not to smile, and once recess came he followed after Crystal

"I will kill you!"

"I thought I was not meant to be talking to you?"

"You're not, so shut up and die silently"

Crystal laughed and walked to a small wall, firmly sitting down to it, patting the space beside her, while taking out her lunch box. Peter sat behind her and lent to her back, he smiled looking up at the clouds

"You know... it's been a while since I felt like this"

Crystal looked at the assorted foods in her box and murmured off-handed way "like what? Happy?"

Peter just continued looking up "I suppose so yeah, I don't really get along with people here, so I suppose happy is a good enough term for what I am feeling"

Crystal poked at one of her eggs "I don't really get why you don't get along with people, most of the class seem nice enough..."

Peter shrugged and took a breath " I dunno, a few days after joining here I was told my cousin would be looking after me, I guess I wasn't the nicest person to be around at the time, Also I have these weird coloured eyes... that could be the reason?"

Crystal looked back at the blond

"And that's why they bully you?" she said in disbelief

"Well it's the only reason I can think of" He replied

She shook her head as she raised some noodles "I honestly don't think that's a good enough reason you know"

Peter smiled and shrugged his shoulders again "it doesn't really matter anyway, not really." 'After all, they are all nothing but worthless maggots that-'

He gripped his head, it was that voice again, and he didn't want to hear it, not now that things were good

He only then tuned into Crystal speaking "... one of the girls in there, Amy she said that you used to smile a lot at the start, but then you had a fight with Thomas."

At that he tensed up, Thomas again, it wasn't as though he had ever done anything to Thomas, but the boy seemed to hate him from the start, and he seemed to know his cousin too.

"I should go get my lunch. We can talk later Crystal"

The change had been nice, but just the mention of Thomas brought him back to reality, this feeling, what he was doing, it was not meant for him, not yet at least.

He retreated inside but looked back to the girl he left sitting on the wall, it was clear he had upset her, but then again maybe that was for the best too, he was not meant to have friends after all.

--

Going back into the class room, Crystal found herself looking right into the eyes of the class president, Thomas had a set face on him and she thought about turning around just to avoid looking at him

"What do you think you're playing at?"

She looked genuinely confused and looked over her shoulder and then back to the boy in front of her "I don't really know what you're talking about..."

Thomas slammed his hand on the table and glared at Crystal

"With Peter, don't play ignorant! I told you to stay away from him didn't I?"

Now Crystal was not confrontational as it stood, but there was something about how this boy was acting that got her back up

"Oh I remember you saying as much, but I decided not to listen to you"

She was ready for the fist that came swinging for her, and she evaded it with a clumsy grace that nearly set her falling over a table

"What is he to you anyway, it's not like you can order people not to be his friend"

"I can't but..." The door opened behind them and Sharon entered, she looked at them both before walking to her desk without saying anything.

Crystal followed suit and returned to her desk, but she was staring at Thomas till more people entered

Peter didn't talk to her for the rest of the day. And he didn't smile either.

Chapter 4

Joys ever fleeting

Peter got ready to go to school, he had a grin plastered to his face that he could not get to back down, and he knew exactly why.

Since Crystal had joined what barely three weeks ago, she had successfully befriended Peter, made him laugh in school, and got them both sent to detention, and made other people start talking to him.

Peter was placing a strap over his shoulder as he grinned to the thoughts of Amy gripping his hand and dragging him away from Crystal saying that Victor's fan-club would be out for his blood if they knew how close he had gotten to the girl.

Just thinking of Victor made him laugh really hard as he pictured the scene that followed after, Crystal being tailed by the older boy and force fed from his lunch box, all while the fan-club hissed from a distance. Peter couldn't tell what had changed, but something clearly had.

He opened the door to his room to look right into eyes that rivaled his own.

Megan was glaring at him, she was only slightly taller than Peter, but there was something altogether menacing about the way she blocked his path with her hands on her hips.

"You're very cheerful this morning"

Peter felt a chill pass over his shoulders, and the smile he had been struggling to erase now faded like a distant memory, He made a move to walk past Megan but she blocked him again.

"I have to go to School…"

"Yes, that's what's bothering me. You are never happy to go to school. You're hiding something from me."

"It's nothing, were just getting to dance today. You know I like dancing, that's the only reason…"

He couldn't look her in the eyes as he said it, but it seemed to be enough to let him pass, when he was at the bottom of the stairs he heard her shuffle into her room and close the door.

Readjusting the bag upon his shoulders he took a step out the door, closing it firmly behind him

--

Peter found Crystal in a bit of a bind, apparently she was getting too close to Victor and 'overstepping the boundaries' it was not as though Victor knew anything about this of course, and it was not as though Crystal had asked him to hover around her like a lost puppy.

Peter came over to them and they turned on him instantly.

"And you!"

"Yeah just who do you think you are getting so close to the girl Victor chose, it's not like you're in his league"

'That's true, I am way beyond him'

That voice rang out in his mind again, and he frowned a bit before answering the girls.

"Um, she is just a classmate, we aren't close or anything, so you can relax. Anyway..." He looked to Crystal "the teacher wants to see you..."

Crystal pushed past the group and rushed off with Peter in tow

"How long have you been trapped like that?"

"Has to be more than half an hour, I got here early cause Aunt Claire asked if I could drop her keys to her, she left them behind and needed to open the shop"

Peter stopped and looked at her.

"What shop?"

She smiled and shrugged, it was nice that he was taking an interest and she was not going to pass up talking to him more, so she answered him while she continued walking

"She helps in a bakery in town, she opens shop and prepares the ovens, but she only does mornings, so it's ideal for her... Why do you ask?"

"I just never imagined her as the working type... I dunno why... Oh, that reminds me, I am taking you into town today"

Crystal opened the door to the classroom; she was looking back at Peter when she entered so she did not see what was in the way

"Going to Town but...Uff!"

She walked right into a table that was being pushed aside by a quiet boy named Cody, Peter who didn't expect the sudden stop, collided into Crystal's back, sending them both sprawling over the surface.

Laughter erupted from the class and two very red teens scurried away into a corner. Sharon was now looking at them like they had offended her personally.

She marched over to Crystal and glared at her, she cast a look to Peter and then turned her direction back to Crystal again.

"You're late, I need you to help clear the floor, the tables need to be stacked and the chairs all folded"

"Alright... Come on Peter"

Sharon's brow furrowed deeply as she watched Peter smile and follow, this just did not make any sense to her, Peter had always snapped at them or ignored anyone who tried to make a connection to him, and this girl just shows up and it's like a whole different person took Peter's place.

Her green eyes trained on the blond, she didn't even notice she was staring till another girl in her class named Karen spoke beside her.

"It's weird isn't it"

"Yeah..."

"You remember when Peter first got here? He was like he is now, only better I guess. It was like really weird when he detached himself from everyone."

Sharon stopped looking at Peter as Crystal pushed him into a girl named Helen, the girl in question going wide eyed and blushing redder then a ripe strawberry.

She gave Karen a questioning look and then sighed before turning her head to see how everything else was going.

"You know Karen... I am tired trying to figure out how boys think..."

"You can say that again, but he does have a cute smile. Maybe if Crystal can train him to be nicer, I might go for him."

Sharon whipped her head around to her friend and snorted.

"What! I thought you were going to ask Thomas out!"

Karen frowned and went a bit red herself...

"Yeah... well... that's not going to work out"

Karen strode over and promptly slapped Crystal on the arm and shouted at her to apologize to Peter and Helen; Sharon calmly watched the interaction with a hint of a smile, before looking over to Thomas.

If looks could kill Peter and Crystal would be dead ten times over, she had seen what Thomas had almost done the other day in the empty classroom as well, he had made to hit Crystal, full on punch her, who knew what he would have done had she not walked in, but despite seeing this,

She didn't report him, well couldn't, to be exact, seeing as the principle was his father, she was more likely to get into trouble for making things up, she would most likely lose her place in the class committee too.

She frowned again and was about to walk over to ask why he hated Peter so much, but the class door closing behind her stalled her action.

The drama teacher walk in, in his usual meandering way, she watched as he strode to his desk and lent to it with legs crossed in front of him.

"Alright class, settle down... Apparently I am meant to teach you how to waltz..."

--

The class was structured so they had one hour warm up, two hours lesson, one hour break, and then practice time when they got back.

Meaning Mr. Smith would sit at the top of the room while the students did whatever they wanted.

Crystal was warming up with Sharon, the girls had to help each other with stretches, as the last time they had mixed it up, one of the guys got a bit too handsy.

Crystal had not spoken to Sharon since the first day, so now to have been paired off with her was rather uncomfortable.

Just before the warm up was about to finish Sharon spoke to her, though it was in a soft tone.

"How did you do it?"

Crystal drew her attention away from the wall to look at her

"Do what?"

"Do that" she made a motion with her head over to Peter who was now being dragged aside by Karen.

"With Peter... How did you get him to break out of his shell?"

Crystal looked at Peter for a moment and then smiled softly

"I remember what it was like to be alone, so I guess I can relate to him..."

The alarm rang to signal warm up was over, leaving Sharon to stare at Crystal while Mr. Smith paired the students off.

Sharon held her head down and then looked off to the side "I don't really understand..." but Crystal could only smile to that too.

"Sharon, I don't think anyone can, unless they have felt the same loss as he did. Just try to be a little nicer to him, no one likes to be called names; even if they don't seem to get upset about it, it really hurts"

After a short while Crystal was paired with Simon, there were more guys in the class than girls, so the guys had to take turns.

She looked to Peter as he tried to get away from Karen, unsuccessfully as she gripped to his hand and pleaded with him to show her again, punching poor John when he tried to say he had to dance with her next.

Peter looked at Karen and then to John, Karen fixed her glasses and then leered threateningly at John.

"I don't know the moves yet, and I need a big strong man like Peter to show me, someone like you would be no substitute."

John held his stomach and shook his head, he walked away from her complaining about her being annoying and not worth it, when Karen turned back to Peter, he was suitably traumatized enough to take her hand again.

"Like this... No Karen... Don't put your hand there" Peter for the third time replaced Karen's hand to his Shoulder, removing it from his lower regions "We have to keep a certain distance. Away... No Away"

Karen was not a good student, as she seemed to think away was closer and shoulder was Buttocks. After finally managing to get her into a dip, she hooked her arms about his neck, and he was never happier to hear the bell sound for lunch. He practically dropped the girl and ran to Crystal pulling her out by the hand.

"I am never making another suggestion in class again. That girl is crazy"

"I think she likes you Peter"

"In the two years I have been here she has never shown any interest in me, why should she start now?"

Crystal grinned and poked his side, he pushed her to the side and laughed, his face lighting up all the more for it, a girl passing in the corridor actually smacked her shoulder off a door frame while looking at him, and Peter didn't even notice.

"I think I might have a small idea why..."

--

Peter spent the rest of the day avoiding Karen, he along with a boy named Jack, Crystal and Thomas, were asked to help in tutoring the rest of the class.

Amy was sitting next to Sharon on a desk they had reclaimed from the wall; she was rubbing her abused foot that had been stood on three times by John

"Where do you think he learned to do that?"

Amy motioned over to Peter as he showed Simon the right starting position, and then moved over to a boy named Toby. Sharon had been watching too, Peter had never participated in anything before, so she was finding it hard not to have her focus drawn to him

"I have no idea, when it comes to it, none of us really know a lot about Peter."

"Looking at him now, you would never think that less than a month ago he was a secluded grump. He acting like he did when he joined the school"

Sharon smiled but then it melted into a frown, Crystal's words were playing in her memory, she had never once tried to look at it from Peter's point of view before, and now she could not help but think on the first weeks he had joined.

"But then he realized he was alone... they never did find his mum and dad, I can remember my Mum telling me, that the police suspected him, but when they tried to arrest him, his cousin prevented it, something about him being a child and no solid evidence."

Amy looked at her with crystal blue eyes and then back to Peter

"My Parents told me that he had been in a mental institution, and that the reason his eyes are so vivid is because of all the drugs he had been given. They said that his parents tricked him and left him for his cousin to care for"

Sharon shook her head and then stood up smiling to Amy

"You know... I don't really care about all that stuff; maybe I will try to be a little nicer to him."

Chapter 5

Forget the rules

Peter had not stopped smiling since class had ended; Crystal was just walking beside him constantly asking him what was going on, but he was keeping his mouth firmly shut to her questions.

The dark haired girl was grasping at straw, but he was looking up into the sky. The clouds were looking pretty ominous, and he was about to suggest they pick up the pace when she came up with her next suggestion

"You're taking me to an illicit pawn broker that deals in young girls for the slave trade"

The blond laughed out at this one and shook his head "Nah, I wouldn't make much on you anyway, you're too lazy and need to be babied through things"

"I do NOT need to be babied!" Crystal said in a mock anger, grounding to a halt and folding her arms.

"Oh right…" Peter turned to look at her and then shook his head "That's why I had to be your partner for most our lessons"

She went red and then scrunched up her face

"Well... You..."

Peter laughed and beckoned her to keep going

"We're nearly there, let's go before the sky opens up"

--

Peter's house was an unassuming type, the area was quiet, and it was a two story with an attic conversion.

He had told Crystal to wait outside, that he just had to get something he had left behind, and he wouldn't be long, but as Peter approached the door, it opened.

Megan was standing at the door, and Crystal noted that she could not have been that old, she was slightly taller than Peter, she was slim, had a rich copper color to her hair, but her eyes were startling, the same green of Peter's minus the light behind them, she seemed pleasant enough when she smiled to her, but it was when they looked over to Peter that they turned sharp, there was something about that look that made them colder.

At least till she smiled again.

"Peter! You never told me you were bringing a friend home!" Her voice was like a bell, and it was pleasant to listen to, but Peter knew it was an act, Crystal of course couldn't have known and walked up with her hand stuck forward in greeting.

"Hi, my Name is..."

"Crystal, I know, Peter has told me all about you, though he has not shared what you were doing on the weekend... Care to enlighten me?"

Peter's jaw had dropped and he had gone pale, He could not see how she could have known her name, let alone that he was with Crystal on the weekend.

Crystal however seemed un-phased by her knowing this information, perhaps Peter had shared it, though the look on his face said otherwise, so she decided to play it cool and off-putting, considering how Peter had talked about his cousin in the kitchen the previous weekend..

"Nothing really, I needed a dance instructor, sort of roped Peter into it. This is the last weekend before the dance though, he seems to think we need something in town, a bit of a waste of my time really, but who am I to complain? After all, I suppose I am lucky enough to have someone teach me... even if it is Peter. No offense, but we don't really get along to well."

Megan's eyebrow lifted slightly, she had not expected that answer, Crystal however just smiled stoically, looking right into her eyes as she continued to examine her.

It seemed that she passed the test as Megan then turned to Peter.

"Alright, you go get what you need, I take it you won't be home tonight, should I expect you tomorrow?"

Peter, who had been staring at Crystal, turned his gaze to his cousin. His eyes had lost the shocked look and returned to the nonchalant gaze she was used to seeing.

"I will head to my classes from her house... I'll be home after them"

Only then, did Megan clear a path for Peter to enter, shifting her hip so that she was leaning to the door frame, he moved past her and she flicked her hair over her shoulder as he moved up the stairs

"So... Crystal, how long have you and Peter been friends?"

He trotted up the stairs as fast as he dared, after her performance he knew Crystal wasn't about to tell her that they were friends, but the thoughts of the two of them chatting made his skin crawl.

He hurried into his room and upended his mattress to pull out bag he prepared the night before, it had all the things he would need for his classes the following day, it also had a note he needed for the surprise he had planned.

As he came down the stairs he could hear Crystal calmly speaking to his cousin.

"Well I am an easy going person, I can't say Peter is the same, though I did try to befriend him, he didn't seem taken with the idea, insisting that he would teach me the steps I need to know, and that would be the end of it. I have to admit, I do feel a bit sorry for him... but I can't force my way into his life."

Megan smiled softly and then lent into her for a moment "Trust me, you're better off not knowing Peter. It only ever ends in trouble."

Before she could question that statement, Peter pushed past Megan and looked to Crystal

"Let's go"

They were the only words spoken between the two for a long time, even standing at the bus stop there was silence, Peter kept looking over his shoulder as they were walking, and it was only as they were getting off the bus that he spoke again.

"What did she say to you?"

"Nothing much, just asking how long we had been friends, things like that"

"What did you say?"

"I said we weren't friends, and that you only wanted to teach me dancing, and nothing more than that" Crystal gripped to the blonds hand and forced him to turn and look at her.

"Peter, what is going on? I don't really understand why it is so bad to be your friend. I know I denied it and all, but that was... well you were so adamant before about us not being friends, it seemed like the right thing to do at the time. But seriously I don't see how..."

Peter placed a finger to the others lips, and it effectively silenced her. He didn't speak for a while, but just walked on; he seemed to be thinking about something.

"Crystal, you know, the only place I have to act that way, is in school, everywhere else I get to be myself, hang out with people, laugh joke, you know, normal stuff." He said this in a soft tone that drew her in and begged her to pay attention

"I don't know why it's that way, and I never got an answer when I asked. The only thing I was ever told was that in the other classes they don't really know who I am, so it would be easy for me to vanish. Seeing as they can never know my full name or my address."

Crystal frowned as he said that and before she got to ask the question, he answered it for her.

"I don't really know why I would need to vanish to be honest, my parents used to move around a lot when I was small, and the only relative that ever came to each place was Megan, but I never thought too much on it, this time though, it was only Megan that came, and we have been in the same place for four years."

He almost sounded defeated as he said it, and you could hear, almost feel the pain in his words.

"But I am not allowed to stand out at school or get to know the people locally, I thought at first it was just Megan being paranoid, but recently whenever I would make a new friend that gets too close to me, or if someone finds out too much about me, something bad would always happen to them, and then it would be blamed on me."

He stopped walking for a moment and looked at her.

"I don't want to make new friends, because I have to stay out of trouble. And you know, If something were to happen to you..."

Crystal looked stunned and Peter shook his head, he knew that it was all a bit... incredulous, but this was his life.

They walked on in silence for a while more, the clouds hadn't opened up yet, but the air was getting heavier so Peter knew it would start raining soon, he reached into his bag to pull out an umbrella as Crystal began speaking again

"You know, Thomas said something to me that I didn't understand when he told me not to get close to you, I said he couldn't stop me and he said *"I can't but..."* ... but what? Someone else can?"

She was looking worried as she continued "Peter, What's going on with you? Why are they doing this?"

They were turning into an old fashioned building as she said this to him, and he took three deep breaths before stopping halfway up the steps.

"Crystal, about four years ago my parents disappeared, before that as I mentioned, we would travel around all the time, My mum was a scientist and my dad was her assistant, I don't know what they studied, but as I got older they seemed to be more and more protective of me. Megan used to come over a lot to talk to them about things, and a few times she would argue with them."

He looked up to the roof of the building as though he was trying to find something, but eventually he looked back to her, the look in his eyes was one of deep sadness, and his voice echoed it

"After they disappeared things got bad, A kid in class I had made friends with fell from a tree and broke his legs, or at least that was what he told people, a month later he and his family moved away, I found out it was Thomas who did it, and well, we got into a fight, but in the end the blame was pinned on me, I don't know why they are doing it, or even who 'they' are, but I think they are the ones that took my parents, and if I am not careful, they might turn on me, so... Just trust me, okay?"

"Peter..."

"Peter!"

He whipped his head around to see a lively young red head bounding his way; she stopped in front of him and then looked at Crystal.

"So this is the girl you told me about, well I have them ready for you. The director stressed that nothing should happen to them. Also I need to know the other girls waist size. I have to say, you must have pulled some strings to get her to agree to letting you borrow them."

Peter shrugged and then smiled in a hollow way

"Nothing much Susan, I just finally agreed to play Puck in 'a mid summer nights dream' and Karen... I would say she is a 30 inch waist. 38 hip, not that that matters, and she has about a 38 to bust."

Crystal frowned and then laughed. Susan frowned too for a moment and then bid them to follow her. Crystal nudged Peter and mouthed 'you're taking Karen to the dance?'

He grinned and nodded mouthing back 'She is terrifyingly forward'

Susan lead them both into a props room, there was a dress bag and a suit bag hanging ready for them, each had name tags upon them.

Peter followed Susan along the lines of clothing and left Crystal as she marveled at the area she was in.

There were so many costumes, it was amazing, it was clear to see that Peter was part of this drama group, though judging from the fact that he had to be bribed into playing a main part, he didn't take part so much, but he was pretty talented, enough so to warrant a favor.

Peter was coming back with a dress bag in his arms and he was smiling, Susan was pulling on his arm.

"Peter, do the lines! I will play the fairy!"

He looked at her dubiously

"Please?"

The girl was begging and it worked as Crystal found
the dress bag Peter had been holding bundled into
her arms as he hoped atop of a chair, one foot up
on the back of it, he raised his hand so it peaked his
eyes and he made as though to search for
something

"How now spirit! Whiter wander you?"

Susan danced on her spot and began reciting from
a script in her hands, though in a stiff manor

"Over hill. Over dale, Thorough bush. Thorough
brier, Over park, over pale, thorough flood,
thorough fire, I do wander everywhere. Swifter
then the moon's sphere; And I serve the fairy
Queen.
To dew her orbs upon the green, the cowslips tell
her pensioners be: In their gold coats spots you
see; those be rubies, fairy favours, in those freckles
live their savours; I must go seek some dew drops
here, and hand a pearls in every cowslip's ear.
Farewell, thou lob of spirits; I'll be gone: Our queen
and all her elves come here anon."

Peter tilted the chair forward, causing him to land
in a drop before the girl, Crystal noticed how red
she went as he lent in close to her, lowering his
voice as though he was bidding her warning, his
voice became like silk and Crystal found her breath
had stilled as she listened to the poetry Peter spoke
as though it was his everyday speak.

"The king doth keep his revels here to-night;
Take heed the Queen come not within his sight.
For Oberon is passing fell and wrath, A because
that she, as her attendant, hath A lovely boy, stol'n
from an Indian king;
She never had so sweet a challenging:
And jealous Oberon would have the child,
Knight of his train, to trace the forests wild:
But she perforce withholds the loved boy,
Crowns him with flowers, and makes him all her
joy:
And now they never meet in grove or green,
By fountain clear, or spangled starlight sheen,
But they do square; that all their elves for fear,
creep into acorn cups, and hide them there."

Susan's face was a blank, and Peter took a step
away from her, it was only when crystal swallowed
loudly and then made an attempt at applause,
though with a dress in his hand it was not so much
an ovation as a muffled clap.

At that Peter turned to look at her and smiled
brightly, it was almost like he WAS a different
person, even his features seemed changed, but as
he pointed a finger to Crystal, his features began to
melt back to normal, but he continued speaking
with this melodic accent

"And you good Lady.
Should any word escape from thy lips pertaining to this night,
I would bid thee to flee hence from my sight,
This favor that I offer you, it harbors malcontent.
For if one word you speak on it, I shall see your life be spent"

She laughed slightly nervously and then whispered to him... "What does that mean?" He grinned and whispered back "tell anyone about this and I will kill you!"

--

Aunt Claire threw her keys to the side counter as she came home that night, she had been out with a friend and had brought home take out, seeing as she had not had time to cook.

She knew that Peter would be over so she had gotten extra, so she supposed she should not have been too surprised to hear him when she came home, but the words being spoken made her blood run cold.

"Oh come on Crystal, women have been doing this for years, it can't be that bad"

"Oh yeah, you try having your insides being forced up through your rib cage and then say it can't be that bad!"

Claire almost threw herself down the hall to stop whatever was happening, only to burst out laughing as she looked at the scene.

Crystal was trying to get away from Peter who was holding up a corset to her, and she had a look on her face as though Peter was trying to kill her.

Peter looked up from what he was doing to meet the shocked and slightly reddened face of Crystal's auntie.

"Can you please tell her to try this on?"

"I'd feel like a right twat in that, not to mention not being able to breath"

Claire laughed and walked over to the vintage dress that was hanging up on the kitchen door

"Where did you get these?"

"Peter got them."

Peter who was dressed in a light grey suit smiled to Crystal's auntie and then held out a hoop for her to put on, the dress itself was a pastel purple with silver threading, it had a flower design embroidered on the bodice and what looked like lace and crystal trimmings.

"I really don't see how this is necessary"

Peter sighed and flopped down on an armchair

"Hey, if you don't want Victor to win this popularity contest, that's fine with me. Just hope his fan-club are alright with that"

"And just how will me being uncomfortable help him win?"

He laughed at that and shook his head.

"Crystal, it's not just about how you dance, it's about how you look, the costume you get, the effort you put in. Victor always takes the nice looking girls to this thing. It was a girl named Alice last year, but she lost out to Johnathan and Susan. Because Alice didn't wear feathers in her hair"

"Feathers?"

"It was a cowboys and Indians theme last year"

"What did you go as?"

"I didn't"

"Then how did you...?"

"Everyone knows about it, if Victor loses, his groupies let the world and its dog know about how it was in no way his fault, as he is perfect. And as for the girl, well Alice was so badly bullied she moved schools not long after."

He was looking at her as if this was obvious, and began to advance on her again.

"Anyway let's lace you up, you have to get used to moving in this, I am going to show you one more set tonight, and tomorrow we can relax, okay?"

Crystal frowned but did as she was told, after getting help with the dress and begrudgingly the corset, she followed him down to the basement. The set they were learning was an easy one, though one not covered in class.

It seemed that Peter had a plan to give Crystal an unfair advantage, doing this move would make them stand out a bit more and give them a better chance at getting votes.

The basic move was that two couples would be circling each other, hands linked high over their heads. T

hey would split and then turn in co-ordinance, switching partners as they did so, he told Crystal not to worry, as he would show Karen and Victor the dance also, so it would work.

At the end they would bow to each other, and then draw close. And so the dance was complete.

She was a little slow on the turns, and she sometimes mixed up her feet crossing, but all in all, she was passable.

They danced in their outfits for an hour, and then a further two hours out of costume. A light sweat had broken out on Peter's brow, but a heavy one was upon Crystal's.

Peter looked to her as she stood bent over, with hands to her knees, heaving heavy breaths. He then clapped a hand to her shoulder and almost sent her flying.

"I think that is enough for today. You pretty much have it, It took me a while to learn this dance; you did great to pick it so quickly"

She just smiled at him and straightened up a bit, it was getting late, and already the smells of supper drifted down to greet them, Crystal straightened herself out and tried in vain to fix her bedraggled hair, this causing Peter to push a lock behind her ear with a chuckle.

"Let's head up yeah?"

--

Supper had been short, as had the time in front of the television. Crystal seemed tired, He was too of course, but then he was used to these sort of workouts. He had been the first to shower, and was now waiting in the room while Crystal was washing.

He looked out the window, a storm had picked up, it was raining heavily and there was some thunder too, Peter hated thunder, something inside him repulsed to it, the electricity in the storm however thrilled his skin, making the hairs stand on end.

He lent back against Crystal's bed, staring out the window. So lost in thought, that he did not feel the girl climbing onto the bed behind him.

It was not until she was leaning over him that he looked up and even then his gaze was heavy lidded. She smiled and lent a little closer to him before saying

"I guess this is the last night you will be staying over huh?"

He opened his mouth to speak, but the words he should have spoken formed a hard knot in his gullet, wishing not to be uttered, He found himself looking into her dark eyes, and the world seemed to be drowning around him.

He felt his body shifting, he turned to face her and he felt his heart racing, oh he knew what he was about to do, and he knew it was stupid, yet here it was, and she was not pulling away, though the moment he was about to make contact, that voice came again.

'do it'

At those words he froze, half lidded eyes were now open and alert, he couldn't, he wouldn't do this, had he not repeatedly told her after this it would be the end.

"Peter?"

He stood and moved to his own bed in silence, not looking back. He heard her getting up, heard her moving towards him. But still he did not turn around, afraid of what he might see.

She however, gripped his shoulder and turned him to face her. She placed a hand to the blond boy's cheek and lay a soft kiss upon his lips.

Peter's shoulders eased, and he sank into the kiss that was given to him. There was no heat to it, no passion. It was just comfortable, at least till the jolt of pain in his stomach, it seemed as though she had felt it too.

As they bolted apart they both stared at each other in shock, and inside him he could hear the laughter from the ever present voice and an odd sensation trickled over him.

'finally' it said, and a strange feeling of fear flooded him that he had never known before.

As for Crystal, she was clutching to her chest, yet while he looked at her, there seemed to a glow pulsing about her.

It was odd to say the least, but before he could say anything, she turned away from him and went to bed.

Chapter 6

The next day

Peter woke up earlier than Crystal, he had spent a good deal of time looking to the girl as she was sleeping. What had happened the night before was strange, it was like nothing he had ever experienced before, not really.

And he felt odd now, like he didn't really belong, not as in the house or in her room, but more like, he was different in general and didn't belong at all, anywhere.

He had never really felt like an outcast before, it had been forced upon him, but he never truly felt it, but now?

Now the world seemed alien to him, and he had the strange thoughts of his cousin Megan and something she had said a long time ago to his father 'and what happens when he figures out how different he is?'

The conversation had died there, as they had spotted him, and he was too young to question it at the time, but now that he remembered, he wanted to know... just what was it about him that had her so...

But the thoughts of his cousin brought another mind. Megan had known about Crystal. Even though he had said nothing to her, she had known where he was, and the name of the person he was with.

The blond swallowed hard and looked away from the pale girl. He had to end this... this whatever it was before it went too far.

Upon dressing himself and gathering his things, Peter made his way downstairs. Claire was preparing breakfast, on seeing him she gave a huge smile, one that then faded slightly as she realized he was going.

"You're not staying for something to eat?"

"I am afraid I can't, I have to get to Karen's house this morning and then I have classes later"

"But its Sunday!" She pleaded as though that made all the difference

Peter smiled to her and chuckled warmly, "It was truly a pleasure meeting you Ms Li, I appreciate you having me in your home"

As Peter turned to leave he heard her ask "will you be coming before next weekend?"

To that he just shook his head before leaving, he didn't want to draw it out anymore then he had to, knowing Crystal wanted him to stay was one thing, but to have her aunt asking him to stay also, it was hard to turn away from, but strengthening his resolve he closed the door behind him, and the soft click of the lock was almost deafening to his ears.

--

It hadn't taken long for the depression to set in after leaving, and even though the trip to Karen's wasn't far, it felt like an eternity away, had never been to this side of town, so the unfamiliarity made it just a bit worse.

He got off the bus and looked at his phone, still another fifteen minute walk, and only a few houses in sight.

Karen's house was... well it was a mansion! Why was she even in their school?! She could have had private tutors every day, she didn't need to go to a school at all.

As he reached the entrance he looked up to large gates and faltered, what was he supposed to do? He could not see a bell nor any kind of intercom. But before he had to question again the gates opened in front of him.

Peter froze. Looking around him to see if there was someone there, but there was nothing, no one. Cautiously he began to walk towards the house.

Though describing it as such was a bit of an understatement, this place was vast, and his legs felt weary as he began the assent up the stairs before the door.

Marble pillars reached to a high roof, each carved with intricate ivy designs, and it was as he investigated these that he was caught into a bear hug.

Karen Latched onto his side and began dragging him into the house without so much as a hullo.

The hall was amazing, a crystal chandelier dropped down over spiraling staircases, Karen took his hand and linked it in hers before tugging it to get his attention.

"Daddy works for the government, so we get plenty of money to make our life easy. But you shouldn't worry too much. I don't care about money Peter. So you don't have to live up to anything. Just adore me and that will be enough to be my boyfriend"

His eyes widened, Boyfriend? He had never agreed to this! Sure he said he would take her to the dance, but, Boyfriend? He felt her grip tighten to his hand and her smile grew.

Peter had never had this kind of attention from a girl before, and for this to happen, after what happened last night! He turned to tell her that he could not possibly be able to be her boyfriend, but then her father came down the stairs to greet him.

"So this is the boy that you…"

Words fell short from the mans mouth as Peter turned large eyes to look at him, the man was tall, well built, had neat black hair, and his eyes were the same dark of Karen's. He seemed to be a bit taken back when he first looked to him, but after a cough he continued.

"I am sorry, you just reminded me of someone. What's your name son?"

"Erm… Peter…"

The man just nodded and turned to Karen

"Now you treat him nice Karen, I don't want to hear any more stories of broken noses of any other appendages, you hear me?"

"Yes sir" Karen nodded and then turned to Peter as her father walked away. "So where is this Surprise you said you would have for me?"

Peter had been watching the man walk away, and had almost forgotten Karen was there, He looked to her eager face and smiled brightly.

He put down his bag, latched to the back of it had been two suit carriers, he unhooked them and then presented the larger of the two to Karen.

She unzipped it and took a step back, gasping as she did so.

"Wow"

This was the only word she could exclaim as what she was looking at made her a bit tongue tied, before her was a true period dress, it was Ivory silk with a gold embroidered front, the under-dress was a corset and it had gloves and costume jewelry to match.

She gingerly reached forward and ran her hand over it, it felt old, but not in a dingy way, in an expensive way, she looked back to Peter, who in turn just smiled more.

"So do you like it?"

"I love it! But, where did you get this"

He laughed and scratched the back of his head "I know people, anyway, you will need to try it on, if it's not right I can change it today before I head into class"

Karen gripped the bag and smiled back to him, then she frowned. "Class? But, we don't have school today?"

Peter just shrugged "I do a lot of classes outside of school, keeps me busy, but I don't mind, I don't really have many friends to hang out with, so it's something to do"

Karen sighed a small amount and then took his hand

"Well I am not letting you go just yet; you have to help me get this on"

Peter went beat red. Strangely the thoughts of helping her into the dress was different from helping Crystal, and he felt uncomfortable about being in the same room as her as she was changing

"Karen, I-I um, I don't think it's"

"What are you afraid of being in a room with a girl in her underwear?"

"Yes!"

The response was quick and Karen laughed gripping his hand tighter, and he found himself being unable to pull away from her as he was being lead up the stairs, he looked back to his bag left on the ground and thought it the Ideal way to escape this.

"My bag, I have to go get…"

"The butlers will put it away"

"But I have to get to class"

"I will have you driven there"

"Karen there is really no need to fuss over me"

"That's what a girlfriend does Peter, we fuss over the people we are dating"

He felt his blood running cold, but there was nothing to be done as he was led towards the girl's room, down a long corridor and a left turn, he was then facing the third door on the right, he had no idea why he felt it important to remember this, perhaps he was making a mental escape route, but it seemed to stick. Karen opened the door and led him to a bed, there she sat him down.

Peter was still red, in fact his face was so flushed he could feel the heat burning on his cheeks, Karen laughed and then walked behind a screen with the dress, hanging it up by the hooks on the frame.

He watched as her top was sent to hang over the screen, and then her jeans. Now he heard the shuffling as Karen pulled out the under-dress, a rush of relief passed over him as he realized she would not be walking out half naked.

Now it was not that he would be entirely averse to seeing a good looking girl in her underwear, but this was... Karen, he went to school with her for ages, and she had never seemed interested in him at all...

But now she was fawning over him like she had found something special... what he could not figure out was...

"Why now…?"

"What?" Karen popped her head out from behind the screen… "Come here a minute, I need yah to tighten this"

Peter stood and walked to her, and she showed him her back. The laces were loose and her skin was bare, he swallowed hard and began to pull on the strings. While he was doing that, Karen repeated her question

"What did you say before?"

Peter looked away from her for a second, not that it mattered as she was facing away from him, and after a moment, he spoke, but only after taking his usual three deep breaths

"I don't understand why you are interested in me… you never seemed to like me before"

He was tugging away as he spoke and Karen gasped at the last pull, regaining her breath she said simply

"You never smiled before; you have a great smile Peter"

He had not imagined he could get any brighter then he already was, but the heat in his cheeks intensified and he set about completing his job before he disappeared from behind the screen again.

Ten minutes later and Karen was walking out in the dress, and he would freely admit that she was stunning in it, though the glasses did take away from the look.

"How did you know my size?"

"I am good at guessing things like that."

"Oh" she said in a soft voice "What else are you good at?"

He had no warning of it, before he could even register what was happening Karen had pressed him back to the bed, and she was climbing atop of him, skirts encompassing his lower body.

He found his eye line filled with her cleavage, and laying back gave her more leeway, her hands now moved to either side of him, and she began to lower herself down. He tried to squirm away, but this only seemed to encourage her.

"I always imagined my first time would be like this…"

Peter's eyes widened and he opened his mouth to protest, there he found in doing so, the gap was promptly filled with Karen, she kissed him full on and he felt like he needed to get air.

When she finally broke the kiss he felt her hands going after his clothing, and that seemed to jerk him into action.

"Karen, Karen stop!"

She seemed not to hear him

"Karen please, this isn't right"

Still nothing and his zipper was undone

"Karen, I... I don't want our first time to be like this. If we... if we are going to do this, I want it to be special"

That stopped her, and she looked at him with large dark eyes, Peter was glad he did acting classes, she was just looking at him now, and he felt he needed to say more, to get her to move.

"Can we... Date, for a bit first at least? I want to get to know you a bit more... this, well doing something like this should be taken seriously, it's not the only thing I want from a girl, and if you are to be my... my girlfriend, I am going to treat you with respect"

This seemed to hit something with the girl, because she stood and looked down at him with a shocked expression

"Do you... really mean that?"

He nodded, it was a bit of a white lie, he meant it, but not necessarily that he wanted her as a girlfriend.

But then her face seemed to hit him like a ton of bricks, she smiled, but not like he had seen her doing before, it was not fake, a smile placed on just to get boys attention, it was a real smile, full of emotion. He was sitting up now and she gripped him to a hug.

"You're so nice, you're like the only guy I know that would say something like that. How did I never notice you before?!"

Peter gingerly returned the hug, but whispered in her ear during it "I really have to go to my classes Karen, My cousin will be mad at me if I miss them…"

Karen pulled back, she did not seem happy about this, but she nodded, Half an hour later, a redressed Karen and an uncomfortable Peter were sitting in a Mercedes on their way to town.

For Peter it was uncomfortable to be driven like this, and it was clear with how he fidgeted. Yet Karen seemed more then used to the lifestyle, she was more focused on trying to touch him as much as possible without the Driver noticing.

When the car pulled to a stop outside the old theater, he could not get away quicker, though he did give a look back from the steps to call out to Karen that he would see her at school tomorrow.

And with that, he stepped into the building.

Chaper 7

What's said at rehearsal, Stays at rehearsal

"Sooo Peter, you feeling up to some banter?"

A pale boy by the name of Yuki nudged to Peter's shoulder, the teen was the same age as Peter, and had become close friends with him in the years they studied drama together, He was skinny with pale skin and even paler hair, his eyes were ice blue also, which made him stand out in any crowd.

Yet it was because Peter had ignored him that he decided to force his friendship upon him, also Yuki would tell others, 'there's just something about Peter'

Another slap on Peter's shoulder caused the blonds head to snap up from its reverie

"What?" Peter was dazed, he was not really able to concentrate on his line. Two things were running through his head. First was Karen and her advances on him, and second.

He felt the over powering need to go back and apologize to Crystal for the night before. The Boy beside him tilted his head a bit and then shrugged

"Lines Peter, can we go over our lines together, Jeeze, I know you are spacey half the time, but you look like you're caught in la la land right now"

He looked back at his script and then to the boy once again. "Sorry Yuki I- I guess I am just over thinking things"

Yuki's eyes seemed to widen, Peter over thinking things, that seemed a bit odd, he never seemed the over thinking type, or the thinking type for that matter.

He had always just come to class learned his parts, played them well, and then went home, If he was honest with himself, Yuki had always been a little Jealous of him...

"Well... should we start?"

Peter stood and stretched his arm above him, bringing it over his head as he lent to the side, he repeated the motion on the other side, and then stopped halfway through... "What is it?"

"You seem different..."

He reached for his script as he said this and then looked to Peter

"Susan told me that you borrowed some costumes, apparently this is the only reason you're playing Puck... you never seemed interested in doing parts before this."

He raised his hands defensively to the look Peter gave him.

"No no, I just mean, it's like, you took part, but it never felt like you were really wanting to do it, you had no energy about you... Something has changed in you. Did you get yourself a boyfriend?"

Peter's face went red and he looked away

"Why would I have a boyfriend? I-I don't go for boys, I told you that the first day I came here"

"What's her name then?"

Peter looked up and was about to say Karen, but something about it just didn't sit right, he furrowed his brow and picked up his own transcript

"Let's just get this over with shall we?"

Peter took on a playful stance and gestured to Yuki with a flair

"My mistress with a monster is in love.
Near to her close and consecrated bower,
While she was in her dull and sleeping hour,
A crew of patches, rude mechanicals,
That work for bread upon Athenian stalls,

Were met together to rehearse a play
Intended for great Theseus' nuptial-day.
The shallowest thick-skin of that barren sort,
Who Pyramus presented, in their sport"

"Is she pretty?"

Peter ignored the question and continued

"Forsook his scene and enter'd in a brake
When I did him at this advantage take,
An ass's nole I fixed on his head:
Anon his Thisbe must be answered,
And forth my mimic comes. When they him spy,
As wild geese that the creeping fowler eye,
Or russet-pated choughs, many in sort,
Rising and cawing at the gun's report,
Sever themselves and madly sweep the sky,
So, at his sight, away his fellows fly;"

At this point he was grinning madly and making the
sweeping gestures of a bird, he turned to conclude
his part, looking back to Yuki before leaping back to
crouch upon a table

"And, at our stamp, here o'er and o'er one falls;
He murder cries and help from Athens calls.
Their sense thus-"

"How old is she? Is she an older woman? Peter you
Dog!"

"Their sense thus weak, lost with their fears
thus strong,"

92

"Oh or is she younger, is that why you won't tell?"

Peter was clearly growing frustrated and said the
next part with gritted teeth

"Their sense thus weak, lost with their fears
thus strong,
Made senseless things begin to do them wrong;
For briers and thorns at their apparel snatch;
Some sleeves, some hats, from yielders all
things catch."

But Yuki did not relent.

"Oh I know! It's one of your teachers in School!"

Peter frowned and pointed at him

"Look here snowflake, if you don't stop this-"

"Is it Jenny the props lady?"

"I swear to God I-"

"Oh wait! Better yet!! Its Susan isn't it! She has had
a huge crush on you for the longest time!"

"Quit it! It's not funny anymore"

"Oh no wait, didn't you say you lived with your
cousin... Peter you're not in love with-"

"Crystal!"

The white haired boy fell silent and looked at Peter for a moment, the blond was gripping to his script as though his life depended on it, and he was glaring at him like he was going to go for his jugular. And Yuki could only say one word.

"What?"

Peter seemed to have reached breaking point and it all seemed to come out of him in a flurry

"Her name is Crystal okay! I didn't mean for it to happen and I didn't particularly want it to happen either, but she, she just gets under your skin, she's like an addiction, I am finding it harder and harder to pull away from her. You have no Idea what it's like. You! You're alright, you're good with people, I never- I mean, I never looked at anyone that way before, and suddenly all I can think about is how soft her skin feels, or, how nice her hair smells, or how just one little smile from her is enough now to set my heart pounding."

"Holy shit"

"And what's worse, I just left her, After she kissed me last night I just walked out this morning without even saying goodbye"

"Hold up, she kissed you?"

"Yeah, it was my fault really, I mean, I kinda started it, but, that's not the point, it was, it was weird and not right"

"Did you kiss her back?"

"No… kind of? I don't know, it was weird, and I got this odd pain when it happened…" He looked down as he thought about it, it was really strange, but when Karen had kissed him this morning, there was nothing…

"it doesn't matter anyway, it's not like I can do anything about it… I am not allowed to have friends, much less a girlfriend…"

"Says who?"

"My cousin"

"Ha! Like she can decide your life for you! Peter! You need to live your life for yourself."

Peter looked up to see the other boy grinning madly, and he could not help but smile himself

"Well that's not my only problem."

Yuki tilted his head, he decided he liked this new sharing Peter much better than the old I am not going to share anything and just do as I am directed Peter.

"Oh and what would that be?

"Her name is Karen, and she has proclaimed me as her boyfriend"

"Just tell her you're in love with someone else"

"But I don't think I am, I mean, I am, but I'm not, if that makes sense? It's odd Yuki, I mean I think about her all the time, and I want to be around her, but, it's- it's hard to explain, I just feel a pull towards her, that's all... I kind of get the same feeling with you, but... like not in a gay way, just saying"

Yuki laughed and pretended to be offended for a moment before saying

"You kissed this girl and now you're obsessing over her, that sounds like love to me Peter my man"

Peter shook his head a bit and then sat down to the table behind him.

"I kissed Karen too, or more she kissed me... half raped me to be honest" he said with a bit of amusement.

"And I would be lying if I said I didn't feel anything for her either, I mean, she is attractive, she was never interested in me before, so I guess I wasn't ready for her to be so forward, but... I could see myself liking her too"

The fair haired boy sat beside him throwing his arm around his shoulder, he jabbed a finger into the blonde's chest and then laughed

"Your life is worse than a badly screened soap opera, heh you're in love with a girl, but you're denying it's love, your cousin won't let you have friends yet you make them anyway from the sounds of things."

He laughed merrily then and mocked a horrified face

"Next thing you know someone is going die dramatically just as you get close to them, Ha, I better keep my distance from you"

He then whapped Peter on the head with his rolled up script and stood up. He mirrored Peter's stance that he had taken earlier and began to finish the lines that his study partner never got to complete

"I led them on in this distracted fear,
And left sweet Pyramus translated there:
When in that moment, so it came to pass,
Titania waked and straightway loved an ass."

Peter smiled and rubbed at his head.

"How about we go get something to eat Snowflake?"

Yuki laughed and nodded, even though they had gotten nothing done, a break was needed.

--

Crystal said nothing to her aunt at breakfast, and nothing as she retreated to her room once again, a weight had descended upon her shoulders, she woke only to find Peter had left, and though she had half expected it to be so, part of her wished it not to be true.

She had a bad headache now also, and it seemed as though there was some music playing just on the edge of her hearing, yet she could not really tell where it was coming from.

Trying to put that aside, she thought once again about the night before, trying to figure out just how things ended up that way, she was never a forward type of girl, so to just go over and kiss him, in her own room, it was very unlike her.

But then again, was it unlike her? she knew she had wanted to kiss him, after all from almost day one she had thought about it, but, how it happened was not something she expected, when she thought about it, he had almost kissed her first right?

That was what that had been, she knew she wasn't imagining it, she wetted her lips slightly, as though trying to remember how it felt.

But it wasn't the same, and the feeling that flooded into her after, it was crippling, like pure energy had been pumped into her chest, but the thing that struck her as most odd, was the thought she had after

'It's not good to love a trickster'.

The dreams that followed after were strange, she found herself standing in rolling fields of green, on one side of her was a beautiful looking cow and upon the top of a staff she was holding was a Raven, in the dream she would say something to the bird and it would reply to her

'I will find you, now that you have awoken my lady'.

She couldn't make any sense of it, but then again, it was only a dream, the reality she was facing was her feelings for Peter.

She knew she wanted to be with him, but also knew that he was not attainable, he had said it himself, that after the dance, it was over... but the truth was, that it was over last night.

She clutched to her chest and frowned to herself, could she so easily accept that just because it was what Peter said? Over? Just like that? Could ties be cut so easily?

A light knocking came to the door and Claire entered carrying what looked to be a bowl of soup, she sat to the bed beside her and let out a sigh.

The pale girl turned her head to look at her aunt, a bowl was extended to her, and once taken a soft silence filled the air, after a few moments passed her aunt spoke in gentle tones.

"Worrying won't help him... all you can do is wait, and be there for him when he resolves whatever problem it is that he is going through"

Crystal turned to look at the older woman, and then back to her soup. "I just... I really like him" The older woman smiled at her and stood up.

"Don't rush it Crystal, if it's meant to happen, it will"

--

Megan was on the phone when Peter came in the door, she cast her gaze towards him as he entered the hallway, a frown was still placed upon her lips and her conversation lowered to a whisper, he did not stop to try and over hear what she was talking about, nor did she give him a chance too.

She clicked the receiver back into place and followed after the blond, her foot falls were barely audible as she came up almost right behind him, it was just before he got to his room that he turned to face her.

There was something in her eyes that put him on edge. And her words did little to ease his fear

"We have to move next month Peter. I am pulling you out of School in two weeks, get your stuff ready for when we are leaving"

Chapter 8

Brought it on yourself

Leaving? Peter was staring at her trying to process what she said, leaving in a month? But, why? Just who was she talking to on the phone? And why was she so hush hush about it?

He felt his temper rising and his brow furrowed, Megan must have seen what was coming as more words began to pour from her hateful lips

"You brought this on yourself you know? What did you think you could disobey me so easily? After everything I have done for you, and you do this? You think I like to see you moping around the house? You think I like to watch you getting bullied by the other children?"

She hardly paused to catch her breath as she continued

"I have tried my best to keep you entertained, got you all those lessons got you classes, all you had to do was behave and keep yourself to yourself, that was all. But you could not even do that!"

She was shaking her head now and looked rather annoyed. It was almost like she really did blame him on all this.

"Well it won't be so hard after we move, I will change your name, dye your hair, might even get surgery, so no one will know who you are, so you can do whatever you want, see if I care on it-"

Peter gripped her arm and glared at her, she didn't seem so taken with this course of action as she took a hold of his wrist and twisted it painfully, sending him to drop to his knees as he released a soft hiss of pain

"Now you listen to me very carefully Peter, it is bad enough that I have had to live with the likes you for these few years, but I will not tolerate such insubordination from something like you"

Through gritted teeth Peter retorted as best he could. "You-you speak as though you're not living from my money bitch"

His head hit the floor so hard that he had spots in his vision as a result and it left him wondering how she was so strong.

A knee crushed into his back and her breath fell lightly to the nape of his neck before her soft voice whispered dangerously into his ear

"I have no need for your money boy, I was doing perfectly fine on my own till I got lumped down with you. You do not have the first clue as to who I am, or what I am capable of, if I were in your position, I would think on my next words carefully before answering."

Her tone was menacing enough that she hardly needed to continue to get her point across, but the words kept coming.

"I am your guardian, and you are my charge, you do as you're told, and I keep you safe, that is the arrangement, if you want to remain safe. You will do as you are told. Do you understand?"

Peter made no sound at first as the biting pain in his arm and back were flooding his mind and making it hard to breathe, all the while that voice was seething within him.

'just who does she think she is, she has no idea who *I* am, if I only had the ability I would strike her down in a-'

Her knee jolted into him slightly and he gasped, it silenced the voice in his mind and jarred him into nodding and only then did she let him up.

"Now go to your room and get your things packed, fill your rucksack with two changes of clothing and the savings you keep under the loose board at the center of your room, we may have to leave early, so we will need to be ready"

Peter coughed some whilst rubbing his wrist, he looked back to her, and then away, there was nothing he could say that would change her mind on this, that much was evident, but it was all very confusing, why was she so on edge?

And why would they have to leave early? Megan pointed her finger towards his room and he shrunk away.

While he began to pack however, he could only think over her words, or more her choice of words. The likes of him? Something like him? It made no sense, he was just a normal guy right?

A normal guy who admittedly sometimes heard a weird voice in the back of his mind, a voice that seemed to be a bit more active recently, but he was okay with ignoring it.

If he didn't, he might have to admit there *was* something wrong with him. He pulled up the floor boards and took out his savings. How had she even known about these?

But as he thought on it, perhaps he shouldn't have been surprised, she knew about Crystal, she knew about his fights, and she even went on like she knew something about him that he didn't... it was disturbing.

But thinking on all that was not giving him answers, nor would it make him feel any better about the situation, so he just stuffed the money into his rucksack and began picking out all the important things to him.

--

Karen tried on the dress again, this time it was without the corset underneath, it didn't look as good, but it was still pretty stunning, she let her fingers trail along the swirls of embroidery that adorned the mid panel of the dress.

She was admiring herself in front of a full length mirror when her father came in, he smiled to her reflection and she rounded on him with a pout

"Daddy! You should knock before entering my room! I could have been doing anything!"

The older man shrugged his shoulders and sat to the bed, patting the space beside him for his daughter to come and join him, Karen frowned deeply but moved closer to the bed none the less.

"Tell me Karen, That boy... have you known him long?"

The crease in her brow deepened slightly as he asked her the question, and she shook her head slowly.

"Not really... I mean he has been in my class for a few years I guess, but I don't really know him that well"

"His parents? Have you ever met them?"

"Urm... I don't think he has any..."

"Ah…" There was an indiscernible expression upon the man's face, and it was a moment before he uttered "poor lad. What's his second name?"

She seemed to know what he was doing though, as she gave him a very stern look

"Daddy, I don't want you to go snooping about, Peter is a nice guy, besides I am more than capable to look after myself"

The older man simply smiled and shook his head while chuckling softly

"I know pumpkin, but indulge this old man, after all a father is allowed to worry"

"Well… okay, his second name is Faben… But No threats daddy, you scared off my last boyfriend that way"

The man just smiled and shrugged

"I didn't like how he looked at you princess"

It was at this point the older man stood and looked over his daughter with a warm smile that only a father can master.

"You look beautiful Karen. I just don't want to think that anyone would take advantage of you"

Little did he know about his pumpkins action earlier, and possibly a good thing for Peter that he didn't, Karen just flicked her hair and nodded.

"I know daddy, but you don't have to worry about me, I will be just fine"

The man smiled once again and left, closing the door behind him he walked down the hall taking out his cell phone and pressed a number on speed dial with a victorious expression on his face

--

The morning came as he knew it would come. Green eyes glared at the ceiling above him, Peter had not slept a wink, He had packed his bag as he had been told to, and left it to the center of the room.

He could smell the breakfast from downstairs, but he made no effort to get up. He knew he had school to go to, but the thoughts of that now depressed him more than it had in a long time.

To face the people in school, people he had grown to like, knowing he would have to say goodbye to them, if only he had kept his distance from them, then this would not be so hard, if he had not made friends, if Crystal hadn't....

Crystal.

Even thinking the name made his stomach flip, how was he going to tell her about him having to leave? Why had she become such an important part in his life that he did not want to face her, to see the girl get upset, or to see her try to figure something out so he could stay.

Knowing Crystal she would suggest that they live together that, Peter move into her aunt's house with her, but he knew that would not work, not until he was of a legal age anyway... just a few months to go, that was all...

A few months and Megan would not be able to boss him around anymore...

A knock came to his door, but Peter said nothing, the door opened regardless and Megan entered holding a tray in her hands, she sat to the end of the bed and left out a sigh, a strange feeling came over him then, curiosity sprang up within him.

Megan never sighed, and he knew that. So to see her practically slumped on the bed was different to say the least, and her voice was odd when she finally spoke.

"You're not the child you were four years ago, are you?"

The question hung in the air, as if waiting to be answered, but both knew there was no answer to it. Peter sat up in the bed and took the tray from her, as if that was answer enough.

She had made him breakfast, consisting of the most unhealthy food you could think of, but absolutely welcome, rashers and sausages, eggs and beans, three slices of toast and a coffee. Breakfast of champions [sic]

"There are many things you don't understand Peter, things I am not at liberty to talk about with you, I made a promise to your father a long time ago that I would keep you safe, and that is what I am trying to do, but I forget sometimes that you are a growing boy, and you can't see things as I see them…"

She sounded tired, and as he looked at her, he could see dark circles under her eyes

"Last night was our first real fight. I didn't mean to hurt you like that, but it seemed necessary, I had to make you listen to me."

He furrowed his brow but still didn't reply, he instead just looked back to the tray she had given him

"Everything I am doing… is for your own benefit, I just need you to trust me"

Peter was looking to at the plate as she finished, her words of a somewhat apology seemed to be sincere, but he knew better than anyone what she was like, and so when he did bring himself to look at her, he could only manage to say.

"This Coffee is poisoned isn't it?"

And to his utter dismay, his cousin smiled and then even went so far to laugh, she began to shake her head, but stood before she said anything else, there seemed to be a look in her eyes, not quite sadness, more like... defeat.

Her next set of words came out in the serious tone he was used to

" I guess that was a response I should have expected, but regardless Peter, I need you to act as you had been in the last two weeks, Do not tell anyone you are leaving, it is imperative that no one knows about this.

Once we have relocated, I will contact that girl you are fond of, Crystal wasn't it. If I deem it safe, you can meet with her, I see now that you will no longer blindly follow my orders, but perhaps with this incentive, you may be more willing."

She turned to leave, and Peter nearly knocked the tray to the floor in an effort to rise from the bed and stop her, the clatter seemed enough to stall her and she turned to look at him once again, he remained frozen for a moment, but then spoke softly...

"I just don't understand... why do we have to leave to begin with?"

Megan just turned from him then and shook her head saying

"Telling you now would only complicate things, I am not a bad person you know... I am just... no good with people."

He put the tray aside and stood up, he was not about to let it go, he wanted to know just what was going on, she said she promised his father, but she only came after they disappeared, did that mean she knew something was going to happen? That they knew?

She hadn't moved from the door, and he placed a hand to her back to try and get her to turn, but she only seemed to slump and didn't turn to face him.

"No good with people? Megan, you have been awful to me, my whole childhood and nothing, you didn't even help me when I realized my parents weren't coming back, and the bullying at school, your solution was to tell me to shut up and not talk to anyone... it was like you went out of your way to make me miserable."

She turned to face him after he said that, but her eyes were looking to the side, he had never seen her like his, and he almost felt like apologizing but what she said next made his mouth run dry

"I can hear him too, when he talks to you, that voice in the back of your mind. I hear all your thoughts too. That was one of the gifts you gave me. Honestly, I hated you for it. When I was away from you, it wasn't so bad, I could ignore them, people's thoughts were more like whispers."

She looked at him then, and there was a broken look to her eyes

"But then I was told I had to live with you and the power seemed to increase, I could hear thoughts of people across the street as loudly as though they were standing next to me."

"Peter, the reason I stay at home, the reason I keep the television on so loudly, is to try to keep the thoughts out. Humans are disgusting two faced horrible creatures, they lie to you with a smile on their faces, think the most debase things without even knowing you... do you have any idea the hell I have gone through because of you?"

She looked away from him and frowned

"Well, it's not like it is really your fault, you never asked for it, Even your father was surprised when it happened. But I did hate you Peter... yet you are also my Family... the only family I have other than your parents... so, I am sorry okay... I will try better from now on"

He didn't know what to say to that, it made no sense, but before he could question it she had gone into her room and locked the door, leaving him alone and more confused than ever.

Chapter 9

Awkward

It was all well and good for her to say, 'don't tell anyone we are leaving' but he couldn't just revert back to the boy he had been before he knew this titbit of information.

Not to mention her proclaiming to be a mind reader and blaming him on it, there was just too much to deal with and even though he was a good actor, it was different to pretend to be something you're not in real life.

There was also the problem that he also didn't know what to say to Crystal.

She had kissed him, sure he had wanted to do the same but it was her that did it, and now with the pale raven haired girl sitting next to him he felt like he had crossed some line he didn't even know was there.

Peter felt his stomach squirm and he could not keep his attention on what the teacher was trying to say.

Crystal nudged him and he looked to her in a slight panic, the pale girl just smiled and pointed at his book and then to the teacher, A teacher who was looking very impatient at him.

"Page 42 Peter, start reading"

He stood awkwardly and tried his best not to choke as he was reading.

The rest of the classes followed the same pattern, and it was clear that Peter was spacing out, he was ignorant before yes, but now he was just distracted.

Crystal noticed, but she had an idea; all be it the wrong one, of what might be troubling him. So at lunch time she cornered the blond.

"Peter, I think we need to talk."

Green eyes evaded her gaze and Crystal frowned. It was worse than when they had first met, that time Peter was withdrawn yes, but now, he just wanted to say something to her, but was afraid of what she was going to say to him first.

"Peter please... listen, if it is about the other night. I am sorry okay, it's alright I mean, we are friends right?"

Emerald eyes began to look to obsidian, he felt his eyes widen a touch, he hadn't thought they would talk about it, but then what did he think they would do?

Pretend like it never happened? Actually that was just what Peter had been planning to do, but Crystal was…

"I think we were both tired, I mean, it was silly right? Nothing to get worked up over. So don't worry about it, I am not embarrassed by it. We can still be friends right? Well at least till the dance right?"

Now while she was trying to be consoling, trying to be reassuring, trying to let Peter know that she didn't mind the kiss, that she wanted to be his friend still, what Crystal did not realize was, Peter was reading it in a very different way.

Tired? What did she mean by that? Did she think it was some kind of joke? That putting himself out there like that was nothing! NOTHING! Peter felt himself get angry, he narrowed his eyes and scowled at her, and Crystal seemed slightly confused and a little taken back by the cutting tone that followed.

"Right, Yes. It was nothing, you're right. Now if you will excuse me I have to go find Karen"

Peter practically marched away at double pace, anger seemed to radiate from him, Karen was not too far away from them and others could only watch as he gripped her wrist and actually forced her from her friends, dragging her away from them while saying something they could not make out.

Amy and Helen looked back to Crystal and she shrugged, she honestly did not know what just happened.

Karen was looking worriedly to the blond and then back to her friends. She followed along saying nothing, she had seen Peter angry before, many times in fact, but she had been on the receiving end, well not that it was actually directed at her per say, but his grip was tight and his jaw was clenched, and she dared not to talk to him till he got her into an empty lot.

"I don't see why we have to do this, I mean, it's not like the dance is important to me or anything…"

Peter looked up at her for a moment and then away again, he then talked to the ground, almost spitting out his words.

"Yeah, well, I made a promise, I am not about to back out of it just because… well, I am not about to back out of it. Anyway, I thought we were meant to be spending time together and all that."

"Okay Peter I think you need to calm down"

"I am perfectly calm, why wouldn't I be calm?"

He held his hand out to her and she took it. It was weird, to be dancing out in public, but it was also fun, Karen found herself behaving this time, and Peter was more thankful for it.

30 minutes later and he had calmed down enough to slow his steps and come to a stop. He looked away from her feeling more than a bit guilty.

"Sorry Karen, that wasn't very nice of me was it?"

His dance partner smiled to him and shook her head.

"Not really no" she said "but clearly something Crystal said got under your skin, wanna talk about it?"

Peter's eyes widened and he imagined the conversation, it ended in her being pissed at him for cheating (despite them not really dating).

He stuttered over a few words, but was saved when the class bell rang, leaving the pair to look towards the school.

That was when Peter saw him staring, dark eyes and matching locks, not a mirror of Crystal, but you might think them related if you didn't know better.

Karen began to tug on Peter's hand and slowly he began to follow, staring at the class president till they came practically face to face. That was when he felt his wrist being gripped.

"Karen, tell teacher we are going to be late. I need to talk to Faben."

Karen frowned slightly but nodded, she had not really spoken to Thomas since her confession to him last month, and he rarely acknowledged her at all, so having him order her about like this was irksome, but she couldn't do anything about it, he was the class rep and in truth, he scared her a bit.

Thomas faced Peter; he stared at him until the blond was uncomfortable enough to look away.

"What do you want?" Peter said in a hushed tone that was a reflection of how he had been before he had met Crystal

Thomas merely frowned and let the silence hang for a bit more, Peter looked back up to him then but said nothing, just waiting for the other to reply, but after a minute he felt it was enough, after all he was not having the best morning as it was, yet just as he was prepared to leave, Thomas began to speak

"It's only a few days to this dance; I am beginning to wonder how you will change when it is over"

Peter said nothing but only stared at the dark haired fellow as he continued

"I don't think it is a good Idea for you to be dating Karen, or for you to continue being friends with that other girl."

"Her name is Crystal"

"I don't care what her name is! Peter… you will only get hurt in the long run. I know you don't much like me, but…"

Thomas's hand was cold as he gripped to Peter's, And the sun kissed boy startled to it, taking a step away only to find himself stalled.

"Stop it Peter, you have to stop this, it was better the way it was before, you weren't hurting anyone, and no one was hurting you. It was better being on your own. Don't you understand, she has changed you, this is not who you really are, you don't dance, you don't participate, you are just there, it is the way it is meant to be, it is the way I have kept it for years now, Why are you allowing that girl to-"

"Her name is Crystal!"

Peter pulled his hand away and glared at the other boy, his green eyes seemed cutting and sharp now and Thomas narrowed his own in retaliation

"You think you know me? You think you know what I like? Why? Just because my cousin told you to watch me? You think that makes you understand me?"

Peter spat the words out in anger, and with each word his temper seemed to spike more

"Fuck you! You don't know the first thing about me! You're nothing more than a self-obsessed freak who likes nothing more than having power over people! I am not your fucking puppet and I will be friends with who the fuck I want to be friends with, so you had better deal with that and get a fucking life Thomas! And stop messing with mine!"

And that was enough, Peter spun on heal and marched back into the classroom. He wasn't aware of the worried look that had come over Thomas' face or what was going through his mind.

But in truth, Thomas had not expected the comeback or the sharp look in Peter's eyes, they had fought before yes, but this was the first time Peter retaliated so seriously. Something was wrong.

Peter entered the class room in a storm, and his teacher just raised her brow and waved him to his seat, Crystal leant towards him to ask if he was okay, but he just glared at her and she slunk back away from him.

He was livid, and for the rest of the day, no one dared to talk to him.

--

Megan would be waiting for him when he home, he already knew what she would say to him, something along the lines of,

-she had not asked for much had she? Had she? All he had to do was act as though nothing was wrong? I mean she sent him to acting school right? Surely he could have done that much? But apparently he could not-

He sighed and jingled the keys as usual and when he walked in the door he braced himself for the lecture.

A lecture that never came. She said nothing to him at all in fact, not even a hello, then while he ate his dinner she said nothing. It got to a point where he tried to talk to her, saying things like, how long had she been able to read minds?

Or, was it like hearing them, did ear plugs work? But she said absolutely nothing to him, and Peter had to say what he knew needed to be said.

"I know he called you..."

This seemed to get a reaction from her, though not with words, she just picked up her plate and put it to the sink. She then left the room saying nothing at all.

Peter was growing more frustrated by the minute, it was bad having her yell at him, but for some reason this seemed worse.

He tried to talk to her again later that evening, but for the rest of the night she was silent.

--

And the silence continued into the next morning, a hush ruled over the house, and it seemed infectious as Peter didn't speak all day in school.

He was with Karen at his break showing her the moves again, and this time she was staying late with him for an hour to perfect it.

Peter didn't speak to Crystal, even though she made an effort with him. He just nodded or shook his head before ignoring her again.

For her part, she was beginning to think it was because Peter meant what he said, meant it when he said he would not be friends with her after he had taught her to dance.

But the truth was, Peter was more annoyed by the subtle if not intentional rejection of his feelings. Yet he was not about to bring it up and besides it would be better this way. Make a clean break or so they say.

And that was how it was, right up till the day of the dance...

Chapter 10

The calm before... with the Girl who started it all

The morning light broke through the window, but it was not needed to wake up the pale girl, Crystal had been up from an early hour, and she was now sitting to the end of her bed frowning, all week she had tried to talk to Peter, tried to get some reaction out of him, but there was nothing.

She went over what was happening but couldn't figure anything out. As each day went on, Peter seemed to be getting worse, becoming more secluded, and she didn't know what to do about that.

She knew she was meeting with Peter and Karen a few hours before the dance itself, and later she would meet up with Victor.

Just thinking on him made her think of the day before.

--

She had spent the entire day with him yesterday learning the steps, he was actually rather impressive, he picked them up right away.

Though the stranger thing was that she was not clumsy in teaching him at all, they just seemed to work really well together.

In fact, it had been the first time she really got to sit and talk to the senior, and she found herself asking him advice

"Victor, Peter and I had a fight... I think? I am not really sure, and now he is not taking to me, what should I do?"

Victor looked thoughtful for a moment and leant back on the wall they were resting upon, Crystal would freely admit to looking a bit too hard at the line of his neck right then, and almost jumped out of her skin when he turned to look at her, like she had been caught doing something she shouldn't, but he just smiled and answered her.

"I think I should be jealous, seeing how much you like him, but Peter is a strange one Crystal, he is a lot like you and me in a way, though he has been bullied ever since he got here. Actually I think you are the first person who has been nice to him in his class"

When he said that to her, she smiled warmly, but it didn't help the problem, and he seemed to realize it.

"Crystal, as strange as this might sound to you, seeing as I only know you a short while, I really do care about you, and if Peter is that important, even if it means I lose my chance at dating you, I promise I will help you however I can. But I think he is going through something, and you just need to give him a bit of time."

It was really sweet of him, and when he kissed her cheek she thought her heart was going to burst, it was a similar feeling to the one she had had with Peter, but in a way it was sweeter, more like a beginning than an end.

--

Back to the present and she shook of the thoughts of the previous day, she had no time to be daydreaming over Victor when she only had three hours before she had to leave, three hours to think, but no matter how much she thought about it, nothing was coming to her, just how was she supposed to fix a problem, when she wasn't even sure what the problem was.

She would have asked her aunt, but she didn't want to have to admit to her aunty that she had kissed her friend while she was up in her room, after all she had been trusted to have him up there, so admitting what she had done might ruin the trust she had earned.

Ironically had she discussed this with her, Claire might have been able to tell her right away what was wrong.

The minutes ticked by, and Crystal still did not know what to say, but she was sure of one thing, she wanted to say something, there was a hollow feeling in her chest, and a sickness in the pit of her stomach.

She did not want this day to come, as it marked an end of things, after today she would have no reason to ask Peter to be near her, no excuses to hold his hands or feel his breath against her as they moved together...

The more she thought about it, the more she knew that was something she was now fond of, it was something she was missing, the closeness.

She got up and went downstairs to the kitchen. Sitting up in her room was doing her no good anyway, after making herself some tea she went into the front room and sat down at the piano.

She was never any good at it, her aunt got lessons for her before but nothing ever came from them, still she liked to sit and play the few songs she knew whenever her head got cluttered, so she opened the lid and let her fingers splay out over the keys.

It wasn't long before music was pouring from the piano, and it only stopped when her Aunt entered the room with shocked look on her face

"Crystal, where did you learn to play like that?"

Her aunts voice was quiet and Crystal just looked at her with a blank expression, play like what?

She had not really been paying attention to what she was doing till then, but as she looked down to the piano and started playing again, she almost whipped her hands back as though she had been burnt.

The music she was playing was almost haunting, and like nothing she had ever played before, and what was weirder, it didn't feel like she was the one playing at all.

"I-" 'we are playing together' a soft voice chimed in her mind and her eyes widened. "Aunt Claire, I think I am going mad"

-- ⤳

Claire had brought her into the kitchen and sat her down, making her a fresh cup of tea and trying to calm her nerves, but there was something off about the situation, her aunt seemed to be a bit on edge, and eventually she said

"Crystal? What are your favorite animals?"

129

The question seemed odd, but she answered it anyway

"Cows and ravens"

Claire frowned and asked another one

"And what's your favorite smell?"

Crystal didn't know what to make of it, but answered anyway

"Willow sticks"

This made her aunt shake her head and finally Claire asked

"And where are you from?"

Crystal laughed and said

"Ireland of cours-"

But she wasn't from Ireland at all, and she had no idea why she said it.

Claire just seemed to sigh and drank some tea, nothing was said for a while, and the tension grew with each second, eventually her aunt spoke, and the words seemed weighted.

"Crystal, I have something to talk to you about; though it can wait till later tonight, I promise I can explain what's going on with you, but for now, you should go enjoy the dance okay? Have fun."

Claire didn't say anything else about it, and Crystal didn't push, she had enough on her mind without adding this puzzle to it. So she just drank her tea and got ready to leave.

--

Even though it was the weekend, most of the school was left open, Crystal had arrived early seeing as they planned to do a final practice with each other before people got there, but she was nervous now about seeing Peter, not to mention what her aunt wanted to talk about after.

She passed the main auditorium, the dance committee would be inside decorating things and getting the music set up, so it was not at all surprising that the doors stood open, but she found them imposing now, tall and intimidating.

Her hands were shaking as she moved past the building and made her way to the low wall where she would meet Peter, she would have to talk with him before the dance, but what would she say?

Turning the corner she spotted the boy, sitting there with his shoulders hunched and his head in his hands, he didn't see her come up behind him, and the first thing the blond would know would be a solid weight behind his back.

She leant upon him and closed her eyes, letting out a sigh as she felt the warmth of the boy behind her, Peter for his part, just lowered his hands from his face and stared to the ground. There was silence for a while, but then the soft tones that made Crystal's voice began to speak quietly.

"I miss you..."

She began and with that the words seemed to come to her, as though they had always been there from the beginning

"Even though we see each other, it's like you're not there, and it has made me feel lonely, I feel like I have-"

Words cut short as she saw a figure coming towards them, it was Karen, she was in a pair of jeans and a wrap top, her hair was in a bundle of curls that were messily thrown up in her head, though it looked wonderful as it framed her face, She had no glasses on and it made her features pop, and Crystal found herself blinking stupidly at her...

"You look beautiful…"

"What?"

This was coming from Peter, who had been
unaware of Karen coming, but had been waiting for
Crystal to continue, but the words had caused him
to freeze up, and Crystal felt it and laughed,
understanding exactly what had just happened,
now she could have just ignored it, but this seemed
like a perfect moment to break the tension

"Well she is beautiful Peter, though as I am sure
you know, she does not compare to you, so no
need to take offense"

Karen looked aghast for all of a second, till she saw
the reaction Peter had to this, the blond had
sprung around and flailed his hand at her, visibly
going redder.

"Y-You… You can't say things like that! I-I am a
man, we are handsome or attractive or burly, we
are not-not pretty"

Karen chimed in then

"She called you beautiful my darling Peter, and I
must agree, you really do cut a stunning form…
with your dazzling green eyes and golden hair…"

With Karen now supporting Crystal in her teasing,
the pair of them chuckled as they continued

133

"Not to mention his wonderful muscle tone, my he has a body most athletes would die for, you should see it"

Karen turned to her and gripped her hands looking a bit pale

"Wait!! Have seen him Naked before me?"

"Well not quiet, I have seen him topless, and it is hard not to notice the strength of another person as they guide you about a room in a dance"

Karen seemed to relax instantly and then nodded enthusiastically to this and Peter looked in horror as the two people he was interested in began to discuss his body in front of him like he wasn't even there.

As a result Peter almost didn't hear his name being called and it was rather late that he saw the pale haired boy approaching them.

"Peeeeteeer!!"

Yuki draped himself over Peter's shoulders and planted a kiss to his cheek, this making Peter shrug him off and Crystal look at the new addition in amusement.

"Peter, you never told me you had a boyfriend"

Peter looked at Karen in a panic, but the girl seemed to be finding it too amusing

"Oh so that's why you wouldn't sleep with me"

"Wait what?!"
"What?"

Both Yuki and Crystal said this in tandem and Peter went redder than before and waved his hands as though he was trying to make what was said go away.

"No, No, it was, she was... it's not that, I am not, Snowflake is a friend, he... besides, I am with Karen right, right, and I told you it was, I don't"

All three of them laughed and Crystal felt like things were finally right again, she looked to the new guy and held her hand out.

"Hi, I'm Crystal, it's nice to meet you... urm... Snowflake was it?"

Her hand was gripped firmly and given a good hard shaking accompanied with a grin

"Nah, name's Yuki, Peter just calls me that cause he's a weirdo"

"I am not! What are you doing here?" Peter said while trying not to have a total meltdown, but Yuki just laughed a bit more

"Oh come on Peter? Can't a buddy drop by to say hallo?"

"A buddy Yes, but you? How did you even get here?"

Yuki sat to the wall and held out a script.

"Got a revised script for ya buddy, I know you said never to call over to your house cause your cousin Megan is a looper, but Ms. Carmen was freaking out and I said I knew where you lived and next thing I know I am being packed off to find you and give this to you, so your cousin told me you were here, she's cute by the way"

He then looked over at Crystal and Karen, a smile seemed to be forming and Crystal felt herself smiling back to him without knowing why.

"But you are really stunning looking though, just how did Peter get lucky enough to get you as a girlfriend?"

Crystal turned bright red and Karen's eyebrows shot up, Peter nearly choked and shook his head furiously.

"No no, Karen is my girlfriend Yuki"

With him saying it like that Karen made a squee of joy and there was a look exchanged between Peter and Yuki that told the paler boy to keep his mouth shut about their talk. So Yuki just smiled wider instead and moved a bit closer to Crystal

"Oh, so Crystal is fair game then?"

He said this with a wink towards her, and it was her turn to choke, but a warm weight came across her shoulder and a smooth voice answered

"Not if I have a say"

Victor was beside her now, and as she looked up to him her heart jumped, he looked so... perfect. And he wasn't even dressed for the dance yet.

She could understand now why he had a fan club.

She looked back to Yuki who was feigning disappointment, but then she turned to Karen.

"We should go and let Peter talk to his friend"

She gingerly took a hold of Victors hand and he gave to a squeeze back, as they walked in Victor spoke to her quietly

"You seem to have figured things out with Peter."

She smiled to him and nodded

"Yes, it just sort of worked itself out"

She said while looking to Karen who chuckled, if teasing him was how you would describe working it out, then it worked out.

Victor obviously didn't understand the joke, but he chuckled along anyway,

"That Yuki boy is an interesting fellow don't you think?"

She looked up at him again and then back to Yuki just in time to see him slapping Peter over the head with the script he had held out, she laughed softly and then nodded.

"Interesting is one way of putting it, he seems nice though"

He smiled to her and then looked at Karen

"And you look positively radiant Karen, Peter seems to be having a good effect on you"

Karen grinned back to him with a light blush on her features and Crystal smiled, the girl really did seem to have a thing for Peter, at first she was worried about it, but now she felt like routing for her...

But then what did kissing him that night in her room mean?

She found herself falling into her own thoughts as they walked, just how did she think of Peter? Did she like him more than a friend or not?

138

She would admit that she felt drawn towards him, but as she thought on that, she also felt that way about Victor, and oddly Yuki, and she didn't even know that guy.

She wondered for a moment if that made her some kind of slut, liking more than one guy at a time, but that was foolish, it was perfectly natural to feel like that right?

It was as she was lost in this spiral of thoughts that she came to a sudden stop. Victor was gently pulling his hand from hers and she looked at him in confusion, but he smiled and tucked a bit of her hair behind her ear, causing her cheeks to glow red

"I think it is a bit early for me to be with you while you undress my lovely gem"

Her eyes widened for the umpteenth time that day and she looked at where she was.

"Oh... Oh right, I have to get changed"

Karen was laughing and Victor lent down and kissed her cheek.

"I look forward to seeing you later Crystal"

He left and Crystal felt immobilized, Karen moved beside her and took hold of her hand as an offer of support

"I have never seen him as infatuated before, he really likes you Crystal!"

She couldn't help the bright smile that spread over her then and she looked at Karen

"You really think so?"

Karen nodded and led her into the changing area to get ready.

--

It was an hour before the dance was due to start and they were all in costume, Yuki was still there, he was sitting beside Karen this time, the girl was in active conversation with him, trying to find out as much as she could about Peter.

"So you're telling me that he is playing a part in a play because he borrowed this dress?"

"That's right little lady, he is playing Puck, and I have to say Pete is one of the better actors in the cast, he was a natural from the start, though he never really talked much other than playing his parts, he seemed to like to keep himself to himself with everyone there except me."

"Well yeah he did that here too, until Crystal came along and dragged him out from under his rock"

"I was not living under a-" the blond began to interject but Crystal cut him short

"You were a bit Peter, you have to admit it" Crystal said with a chuckle.

"I just didn't like to talk that was all, nothing wrong with that"

"Well I prefer you like this, you're really fun to be around when you're not all moody"

It was Karen speaking that time and Yuki was nodding beside her. In the short time he had been there you would think that they all had known each other for years, and already Yuki had been on the receiving end of a few punches from Karen.

Crystal finished up her lunch just as Peter opened his. The boy that had just been smiling suddenly went very quiet.

He took out a note that was on the inside and then lifted out his passport and some money that was placed on top of his lunchbox.

Crystal took the note from him and read it out loud, not really understanding what it meant.

"Keep these close with you, it might be tonight?"

"What does that mean Peter?"

The blond boy just shook his head and frowned. He stood then and tipped his lunch out to the bin, he had lost his appetite and it seemed his ability to speak to them.

After a while the group separated, Yuki saying he would stick around and see what this dance was like, and Crystal heading off to find Victor and satiate his groupies that had been glaring at her from a distance.

A few couples had already arrived and Peter began to lead Karen into the function room. The dance would be a few hours long, and after that, who knew what would be happening.

Peter gripped Karen's hand a little tighter, and she squeezed his back slightly, thinking it was just nerves, if she had looked at him properly, she might have noted a slight reddening of his eyes, but he would not cry... if this was going to be his last day with them all... he was not going to cry!

Chapter 11

In retrospect.

Looking back on the situation, Peter pondered on what he would have done differently had he known the full facts. Would he have ignored Crystal entirely? Kept himself to himself? His thoughts then drifted to Megan, when he last seen her, well... he had to admit that guilt was eating away at him as much as the cords were biting into his skin.

He could see the roofs of houses speeding by as he looked out the window from where he lay on the floor of that rusty van he was thrown into... and the dance seemed like years ago now...

--

It felt like the whole room had turned to get a look at him and Karen as they entered, it was a bit uncomfortable but he straightened himself and held his head slightly higher.

If he thought of it as an acting role, it would be easier after all, he tilted his head to look at Karen and he could not help the warm smile from appearing on his features, she was obviously nervous.

143

He un-looped his arm so he could take hold of her hand, she looked up to him as he did this and he smiled a little wider to her, this seemed to calm her a bit and he began to lead her to the photo booth.

The dances always seemed to go in a certain way. Photos would be taken of the couples and then they would go to the main hall.

They would have dinner or refreshments and then they would start the dance, the first hour or so would be free dancing, and then there would be the formal dance that was coordinated, and finally they would vote for king and queen of the dance.

This one seemed to be no different, He smiled fondly as he positioned himself in front of the camera with Karen, if anything, and he knew he would have this photo to take with him when all this was over.

Karen was flushed and she griped to him a bit more as the photo was taken. And as for Peter, he felt a strange mix of happiness and a pang of loss for the fact that he might never feel this way again.

There was a gasp behind him and both he and Karen turned to look in that direction, and he smiled as Crystal and Victor entered.

He had seen her in the dress already, but seeing the glow on her cheeks as she looked up at Victor seemed to make her that bit more beautiful.

Victor was wearing a cream suit, it was pale enough that it matched to Crystals dress perfectly. Victor's groupies seemed to be a mix of jealous and in awe of the couple, and Crystal gave them a nervous wave as they passed by, this just caused them to both smile and look disgusted at the same time, and Peter chuckled at the sight.

Both he and Karen went to join them, but before they got there Sharon and her date Lee intercepted them.

"Peter you look amazing! And Karen, just wow!!"

Karen laughed and proceeded to pull down a bit of the front of her dress.

"And it has a real corset too, awesome right?!"

Both Peter and Lee quickly looked away from Karen's busty display with a flush on their faces and Peter smiled to the other guy.

"So you and Sharon?"

He smiled and nodded shyly.

"Yeah, we grew up together, I have liked her for ages"

That seemed weird to Peter, seeing how awful Sharon had been towards him, but he supposed if he had known her nicer side he might have thought differently.

Eventually Sharon and Karen rejoined them and Victor and Crystal came over them a short while after, Yuki managed to get in with another girl he picked up, and he made a beeline to where they were gathered.

"Hey guys! So this is Jane, she agreed to be my date, pretty sweet of her right?"

Peter smiled to her and she stuttered a bit over her words as she tried to say hello. This caused Crystal to giggle and Karen to narrow her eyes, but of course Peter was all a bit clueless to it.

"Hey Jane are you okay?"

"She's fine Pete" Said Yuki as he gripped his wrist "Let's go get some chow"

--

Dinner was formal, all proper cutlery and everything, there was much laughter at the confusion as to what forks they had to use, and even more when the hostess had to give a speech.

Sharon tried to give an opening address but ended up being distracted by her date dropping his fork and as a result smacking his head of the table.

Peter snorted and once more laughter broke out, Sharon glared at him and he tried to say sorry with his eyes, but then Lee himself started laughing and the speech fell apart entirely.

The dance started without much to-do, and Lee and Peter seemed to silently agree that they would support each other during the in formal dance.

He actually pulled the poor boy aside at one stage and began to show him the steps of the dance that they would be doing later, Victor and Crystal were in their own little world together, and all the while Sharon and Karen danced together with Yuki who was proving to be quiet popular.

"I never seen Peter this open before" Said Sharon "He was always such a recluse."

Yuki seemed to be confused about her statement and just laughed.

"Peter a recluse? I mean yeah he is not very open, but he is always helpful in the theater, I mean lots of the guys there love him, even if he is quiet"

For both of the girls this was all hard to swallow, how could Peter the guy who was always angry and sulky, be nice and friendly?

It just didn't seem real, but then as they heard a burst of laughter from where Peter and Lee were practicing, it didn't seem all that impossible.

They moved then to join Peter just in time to hear Lee say "Well it will be different with a girl right?" Yuki was about to correct him when Karen spoke up.

"Of course! It's not like my Peter could ever really dance like a woman"

Now usually that would be a compliment to most guys, but Peter was looking at her as if it was the biggest insult she could have said to him, and as a result of that comment he ended up grabbing Yuki's hand.

The two boys took it up as a dare and strode onto the dance floor and Yuki gave a rather impressive performance of asking the blond to be his partner.

Peter in turn had turned coy and actually feinted a blush, looking away as he accepted the prankster's hand.

They easily covered the floor and Peter made a good woman, but the pair of girls gawped as Yuki lead him with a gentile grace and Peter followed it easily.

Crystal and Victor came to join Karen as the spectacle continued, and Victor seemed to notice something the others were missing.

"They really are two of a kind those two. It's amazing that they found each other"

148

Crystal who had been laughing at the scene calmed herself enough to look at Victor in question, but he just smiled to her and said nothing more on his statement.

Yuki led Peter into a final dip and leaned perilously close to him, a lot of the girls about the room started squealing.

Peter though, he thought enough was enough and ended up pushing Yuki back and striding over to his date with a triumphant grin on his face. Victor was applauding him as they returned and he joked.

"I would think you two were made for each other"

Peter faked puking and Yuki held a hand to his chest in a know it all way

"That's what I keep telling him, he just won't listen to me."

Karen took that moment to interlace her hand to Peters, and glared at the other two dangerously.

"No! Bad friends, you stop trying to gayify my Peter!"

It was clear she was joking as she said it, and it got the whole group, Lee and Sharon included wiggling their arms towards Peter chanting, 'you will be gay, you will be gay'

By the end of it Peter was almost crying from laughing while saying "Stop, Stop! I am falling for Victor! His fans will kill me! It's too dangerous!"

It wasn't long after that that they had to line up for the final dance. Peter told Yuki what they had planned, but he decided to sit it out rather than complicate the final move with an addition of another couple, so they resolved to put the plan in motion.

Each move came off perfectly as the entire floor practiced a well-rehearsed routine, the music was longer then the routine itself, but they were meant to repeat it a second time to see it out, the actual dance that went with the music was a lot longer.

This was where things took on a different role, as planned, Peter, Karen, Victor and Crystal, broke the routine and split rounding each other and then switching partners.

Dancing with Crystal, Peter smiled to her and inclined his head to Victor and then winked, it was all he needed to do to cause Crystal to turn bright red.

It was odd for him, seeing as he knew he liked her a lot, but somehow to him, if it was with Victor, he really didn't mind all that much.

They switched back and now something else happened, Victor whispered to Crystal and then looked at Peter, he switched tempo and broke into a different set.

It was one Peter knew well, he moved with Karen in hand who followed his feet as best as she could, but when Peter looked over to see if Crystal was okay, he was surprised to find she was moving beautifully with Victor.

So much so that both he and Karen ended up stopping to look at them with the rest of the hall.

It was like nothing he had ever seen, and once more it looked to him as though she was radiating some light inside her, and this thought was echo'd by Yuki.

"Wow, she is just glowing, and Victor is on fire!"

As the music drew to a finish Crystal swirled elegantly to a curtsey in front of Victor and he dipped into a bow from the waist, with one hand placed upon his back. The applause that broke out after was deafening, and it took a while for Crystal to realize what was going on.

She made her way back to the group, Victor in tow, Victor seemed a bit sheepish and was all set to apologize when Peter interrupted him with excited praise.

"You were amazing!! Crystal, where did you learn to dance like that!?"

Peter said this and she looked back to Victor who was now getting praised by all his fan and a few others from his class also.

"I really don't know, I have been feeling strange since... urm... Peter, can I... talk to you?"

Peter looked to Karen and she just smiled and nodded, and Crystal took him by the hand and led him outside.

As they walked Peter began to feel the strangest feeling of dread coming over him, and he looked back to Karen as though she would come to save him.

It was almost the same feeling he had when Karen had been leading him to her room, and what happened that time did nothing to ease his thoughts now.

He pushed open the doors and held one for Crystal to walk through, she smiled to him and he felt a bit more nervous as a result, why was he afraid all of a sudden, why did she want to talk to him now?

Then again, they had not really talked at all after he had gotten annoyed at her, but then they had been having so much fun that he had almost forgotten that.

"Peter" she started "About the other night, in my room"

And there it was, green eyes went wide and he felt like running, he didn't know what to say or even if he did, he wasn't sure he should, she seemed happy with Victor and he liked Karen well enough too, that should be enough right?

"I was thinking it over, trying to sort out how I feel, and well... I really like you Peter. I know you said we can't be friends after this, but, I don't want that. I want you to stay with me."

Peter felt himself blushing and he heard that voice in his mind laughing

"What about Victor?" he said to her quietly.

And to this she looked through the door window.

"I like him too, actually a bit more than like him I think... But I don't want to lose you either... I know it is selfish of me, and I am a horrible person for wanting so much. But, can we still at least be friends?"

Friends. Peter felt his stomach drop to the word, he knew he should have been relived, but to actually hear it, it was hard. But he forced out a smile to her and nodded.

"I want to keep you in my life too Crystal, even if it is only as friends"

Laughter erupted in the back of his mind and the voice that he tried to ignore so often spoke out again, clearer this time than it had ever been before.

'Is that it Peter? Is that all you are going to say to the girl you love? I thought you were going to give up your world for her.'

Crystal had turned to head back in, and Peter caught her wrist as she turned, the voice was right of course, he did love this girl, but it was in a strange way similar to how he felt about Yuki.

He thought on the night in her room, he thought of the last three weeks, and he thought of what Megan said.

If he was going to have to leave, Crystal would be the only part of his life he was taking with him, she turned to look at him, and without hesitation he placed a hand to her cheek and leant down to kiss her.

And once more the energy spiraled through them both, but for Peter it was not as painful this time. He pulled back from her and she had her eyes closed, he furrowed his brow and spoke softly.

"Even if it is only as friends Crystal, if that's what you want, I will still give up my whole world for you"

Chapter 12

How it ends, or how it begins

The hall doors flew open and they jumped apart from each other, the sight that greeted them was a very ruffled Thomas and a fuming Karen behind him, Thomas's expression darkened as he saw the pair, and his eyes narrowed as he looked between Peter and Crystal.

It was clear to see that he was angry, his fists had curled so tightly his knuckles were going white and he turned away from them quickly.

"You're wanted on stage, prince Victor is waiting" The words were spat out with a taste of venom, and Crystal actually flinched from them, sure she was not afraid of Thomas, but she did not want to be looking over her shoulder all the time either.

She turned to smiled nervously at Peter, but he was looking at Karen, and it was then that she looked at her too, the girl looked really angry, and it occurred to her then that she had just kissed Peter, Karen's boyfriend.

A wave of guilt hit her and she was about to apologize, but Peter pushed her forward a bit.

"Go on, don't keep your boyfriend waiting"

She seemed hesitant to leave, but Peter insisted

"I will catch up with you later Crystal, at least now we know you won't get killed by his fan club..."

She nodded and walked into the hall, only to be stalled by Thomas's arm, a feeling of dread passed over the pale girl, she half expected a fist to come flying at her, but when it didn't come, she let her dark eyes look into the mirror of her own.

Thomas fletcher was usually quite calm and quiet, it took a fair amount to rile him, but there was something about Crystal that pissed him off.

"Just because I can't stop this anymore, doesn't mean I have to like it... remember that."

Karen was looking to the ground as Thomas just walked back into the crowded room, Peter was confused about what Thomas meant, and Crystal didn't seem to understand it either.

With Crystal walking back into the room, Peter was left alone with his date, Karen. He walked up to her and tilted her chin up, but she looked away to the side.

"I tried to tell him not to come out Peter, I wanted to let you and Crystal talk, but when he asked why he shouldn't go out, I told him you were talking with her, he kind of lost it, I couldn't stop him, I am sorry..."

Peter knew how intimidating Thomas could be, even if he didn't understand why, so he hugged Karen to him.

"It's okay Karen, don't worry. Are you okay?"

He wondered in that moment if he should just tell her he had kissed Crystal, but something didn't feel right.

Karen was leaning to him, and though it was not the same as Crystal, he liked how she felt with him. But Megan had told him that she would let Crystal be in his life... she said nothing about anyone else...

"Karen... When this dance is over, I am going to have to have a talk with you okay?"

Karen looked up to him as he said it and she smiled

"Is it about being in love with Crystal?"

The blond almost choked and Karen smiled sadly

"Yeah I figured as much, it sucks though. I really like you"

Peter looked to the side before he closed his eyes and spoke.

"I can't really say I love her Karen, I mean I hardly know her, and besides, I do like you too you know, I meant what I said about wanting to go on dates with you... but..."

He returned his gaze on her, just taking a good look, she really was beautiful, with the contacts she had in, it meant he could now really see her dark eyes, he had always thought that they were black, but now that he looked closely he noticed they were a rich chocolate brown.

"But?" she said to prompt him to continue. But he just smiled and placed a soft kiss to her cheek.

"I'll tell you after okay? Just remember I do want to be your boyfriend, so don't worry"

And as he said it, he knew it wasn't a lie. And if it wasn't, then just what the hell was he feeling for Crystal?

He guided Karen back into the room so they could see Victor and Crystal get their award.

==
"I guess this was the point that I should have done things differently"
==

Everyone was cheering Crystal on, and Victor was holding her hand lightly as though they had been dating forever, Crystal was smiling and looking at him as she had a crown placed on her head, and she turned to look out to the crowd.

She wanted to see just how angry his fans were, and she wanted to see Peter and Karen, she was not sure if Karen had seen them kissing, or if Peter had smoothed it over.

But there was something about Peter's words that was making her worry too, the way he said them, it felt like she was hiding something from her.

It was as she was scanning the crowd that she noticed something else.

There was something going on near the back of the room, one of the teachers was fighting with a woman, he ended up skidding half way across the floor on his back, everyone who was looking began to laugh, but not Peter, No... inside he felt Sick.

It was Megan, and she was looking right at him, his jaw went a bit slack, leaving his mouth hanging a bit stupidly.

Crystal was also looking at Megan from the stage, she was talking to Thomas who strode forward to Peter and he took three steps away from the class president and frowned hard at him, but it did not stop Thomas from gripping his arm in an attempt to move the blond.

Peter stood firmly against him, and this obviously irritated the raven haired fellow and through gritted teeth he said in a low voice.

"You have to go... now"

"No"

Peter pulled his arm back and started deliberately walking towards Megan, the girl in question stood with a hand on her hip waiting for him, she had Peter's backpack in one hand and her own on her back.

She was wearing jeans and a tight top, on her feet were boots that seemed to be older then she was for the wear of them, her long hair was tied back and she had fingerless leather gloves on her hands.

Peter thought she looked like she was right out of the army, and when he got close to her, the first thing he said was.

"Who do you think you are? G.I. Jane or something? Could this not have waited till the morning?"

Yuki and Crystal had both arrived near him and Karen was also coming over, Yuki laughed at the comment, but Crystal remained silent, Karen seemed angry, but Megan was merely indifferent about it and handed Peter his bag.

"We're going"

Peter threw his bag on the ground, glaring at her, he was angry, even angrier then he had ever been with her before, she just seemed to know the ideal times to upset him.

Though in retrospect Peter reasoned that it would have been worse had she come when he was telling Crystal how he felt, but that was neither here nor there at that moment in time.

All he knew was that his blood felt like it was boiling and his jaw was aching from how his teeth were clenching, he felt ready to snap.

"You can hate me later Peter, but right now we don't have time for this, we have to leave! I don't need you spazzing out on me!"

She gripped his arm the same way that Thomas had, only her grip was that bit stronger, and Peter didn't manage to pry himself from it till they were nearly out of the hall.

"Fuck you!"

He whirled around as though to return to the room, but that was when something he was not ready for happened, Megan placed a hand to his shoulder and when her voice reached his ears, it sounded desperate, almost afraid.

"Peter please, we don't have any time to waste, please trust me..."

He turned on her and frowned, he knew that this was coming, she had told him that they would be leaving, she had even sent him a note telling him that it was going to be tonight.

But he just didn't want it to be now, He looked at Crystal who seemed completely lost, and then at Yuki who was just as dumbstruck, and Finally Karen who seemed to be figuring out what was happening faster than the other two from the pained look on her face, then he returned his gaze to Megan.

"I have to get changed first; I promised that I would return these outfits..."

"Peter we really don't have-"

"Megan, just let me get changed! It won't take five minutes!"

The redhead seemed to relent as she just nodded, Peter pushed past her and Yuki and Victor made to follow him, rounding the corner to get to the locker rooms.

Peter's brow creased when he noted who Megan was now talking to, Mr Smith and Simon were both talking animatedly to Megan and just before they moved out of sight, he noted that his drama teacher was then running their way.

Karl said nothing to them, just waited outside, leaving Peter completely in the dark as to why there one time harmless drama teacher was seemingly in cahoots with his hated cousin.

Peter was fuming as he stripped out of his suit, Victor was leaning against the lockers looking lost in thought, while Yuki was pacing in an irritated manner.

It was only as Peter was about to leave that the snowy haired fellow spoke up.

"So you are just going? Was that what the lunch was about? I mean, I saw you take out your passport and the note saying it was to be tonight? I delivered that message for her, I mean does this make it my fault? "

Peter said nothing but he did spare a glance back to the pair in the room, his feet felt like lead and his throat was dry, he forced a swallow but still entertained no words of explanation, he just looked to them both.

"Peter, Come on! This is a joke right?"

"I don't think it is Yuki"

That came from Victor, the older boy was looking right Peter, he was holding a suit bag that Peter had handed him, and his voice was calm but not soft as it usually was.

"This woman has been protecting you for a while now I take it, but I don't think she has told you anything about yourself has she. I mean about just who you really are."

Yuki looked at Victor and then Peter, Peter had gone pale but said nothing.

"You don't have a choice in this now Peter, and we cannot risk them finding Crystal, Yuki or myself. I would explain things better if I had the time, but for now you really need to go, I will find you after and we can all talk. Till then just know I will keep them all safe okay?"

There was a bang outside the door and next thing Peter knew he was being pulled out of it, to his left was Karl, but there was something different about him, his eyes seemed to be red and his skin was pale, almost white.

Peter stared at him for a moment and completely overlooked the fact that there were men with guns in front of him.

Megan was to his right, and she was holding out a sword, Victor was about to step out when he was pushed back roughly by Megan.

A distinct cry of 'Dood on top of me?' made Peter turn and take stock of what was going on.

Victor was on the floor having landed on Yuki, and Megan was once more griping his arm pulling him away, and Karl was shouting something about 'holding them off'.

Peter found himself running, and behind him he heard what sounded like an electric storm, but he could not stop to look.

He felt the panic in his cousin, the urgency seemed to spread in him, and his legs moved faster for it, he was running flat out and almost didn't notice when Megan was not beside him.

He turned at the last minute to see her laying to the ground, her eyes were staring at him, but there seemed to be no life in them, just a blank stare.

Peter's brows creased and he made to run back to her, but that was when he noticed three darts protruding from her left shoulder, then Simon was standing over her.

Or more like crouching, he seemed wild, beside him was the biggest dog Peter had ever seen, and there were men with guns, they were pointing them at... him!

They were aiming at Peter, a blind panic took the blond, and it was only at the shout from his classmate that he began to run again, but he didn't know where to go, he just ran as though his life depended on it.

Peter felt more then saw a round of darts barely miss him as he was pulled around a corner.

Next thing he knew he was running with Thomas, the boy looked stricken, as though he wanted to be angry, but there was too much going on for him to take any action to it.

They came to a small enough wall and Peter cleared it with ease, then they were running through a graveyard.

Thomas seemed to know where he was going as he dragged Peter by the hand up several long paths and then finally down to a large tomb, he swung the doors open and shoved the blond inside, following him shortly after.

There was no light, but in the dark Peter could clearly see Thomas's eyes... red eyes, just like Karl's... Then without warning he was in pain.

Thomas left his fist fly and it cracked sickly against Peter's Jaw, and through his pounding blood he made out the hushed voice of the class president. And anger boiled once again.

"Four fucking years and then this happens, you just had to go and talk to people, if you just kept your mouth shut we wouldn't be in this mess!"

"ME?! Why is any of this *MY* fault!! And *WHY* have you got red eyes!? Who are those people? Why are they after me?"

Thomas glared at the blond, who could barely make out his silhouette, and he sat down beside him with a rather drawn out sigh

"I told them it was a bad idea to keep you in the dark about this..."

"Told who? What the fuck is going on?!"

"Peter, you don't have the first notion about who you are, do you?"

"Of course I know-"

"How are you talking?"

Peter's words fell short and he found himself very confused about the question, what did Thomas mean? How was he talking? Of all the stupid things to ask, but then more words followed and Peter felt his stomach fall.

"I broke your jaw with that punch, you heard it snap, and you must have felt it too... so? How are you talking? Didn't you ever wonder why after a night of sleeping, your bruises would be clean gone? Or why even after a full day in athletics you were never tired. Did it never cross your mind that you were different than everyone else Peter?"

If he was honest with himself, Peter would have said 'No' he had never thought himself different, he was outcast yeah, but he never thought himself strange.

Well the voice in the back of his mind aside... but as Thomas spoke, his eyes grew dim and dark, the red hue disappeared and they were left in darkness, silence spread between the boys for a moment longer and then words hissed out again

"I was meant to protect you, at least in school, I made sure no one got close to you, Simon made sure you never got into serious trouble by acting the fool and drawing attention away from you, and Karl dissuaded teachers from going too hard on you. And my father kept your files secure.

We could not afford for certain people to notice you. All the while Megan was pushing to have you removed entirely.

Every day she would call the organization telling them it was too risky, and every day she would be told that your father wanted you to be in that school and live as normal of a life as you could, before you got dragged into this..."

Peter just listened; he could not believe what he was hearing, dragged into this? Into what? And what had his father to do with any of this, his father and mother had disappeared, there was no sign of them, people had looked, why would anyone be following his orders?

Peter could not find his voice though, none of the questions burning in his mind would grant themselves release, so the blond was stuck there to listen, without saying a word.

"You know, so many times I wanted to talk to you, just hang out with you, but that wasn't allowed, and I hated it, I hated it more and more as I forced you into solitude, but that was my role, and I had to abide by it, then *she* came along, and did everything that I had wanted to do."

"She went against everything that I had been told not to let happen, and even though I knew I should have stopped her, and could have stopped her, I... I just wanted to see you smiling again..."

Peter felt a dull thud next to him, and in the dark he felt something else, or more smelt it, blood, it scent filled his lungs and he could have sworn to a metallic taste in his mouth.

It was then he noticed that he could hear cracking, and brushing his fingers to the ground he felt the cement below him splintering, the blood was from Thomas's knuckles, and Peter spared a fleeting thought as to the force of the punch that sounded so harmless.

But his mind was to flooded with information to linger on it, everything Thomas was telling him, it didn't make sense, and even if the evidence was pointing to it being true.

He didn't want to just accept it without questioning everything fully. So he rounded on Thomas, his back leaning to the door of the tomb.

He had just opened his mouth to speak when the weight behind him disappeared, and the last thing he saw was Thomas's drained face before the world went black.

--

And that bring us to where we are now. Peter had been thinking over Thomas's words, what he had been trying to say; while they had been choppy and not very helpful, what he had gathered was this, Megan had been trying to protect him, possibly died while trying to do just that.

Thomas, Simon and Karl had all been placed in his school to watch over him and make sure someone didn't get to know him, and... and there was something weird about him.

Peter made to move a hand so he could feel his jaw, but his binding prevented it. He sighed and let his head thump back to the floor he was thrown upon, and that was when a strange pair of eyes looked back at him.

"You're awake"

Peter edged backwards as the man moved from the passenger seat, his eyes were a deathly pale blue, and his hair was mousy brown, but it was the Tattoo that freaked Peter out the most.

On this man's face was a tattoo of indecipherable writing, lines and lines of it, as though a page of a book had been transcribed, he bent down to Peter and edged up the blonds top, he produced a small knife and pierced his own thumb to draw blood.

Peter freaked out and kicked as much as he could, but his bound legs connected to nothing but the man's hand, and Peter found himself forced forward with a graceful sweep of the larger man's arm.

The blood traced over his abdomen, and the strangest sensation came over the blond, symbols began to swirl over his stomach and up his chest.

The voice within him was screaming in pain and though Peter could not see it, his eyes were glowing.

To this the man smiled, this seemed to irritate Peter to no end, pushing forward he felt a desire to bite this man, to tear at his throat with his teeth just to wipe that smirk from his face.

But with a twist of the man's hand Peter felt his power draining from him, a tiredness washed over him and he hit the floor of the van before he registered what had just happened... He would not wake up for the rest of the journey.

Chapter 13

We have to get out of here!

"I'll hold them off!"

That was the call that rang out as the one time lazy drama teacher took a more defensive stance, Victor, who had been forced backwards, now watched with a certain amount of frustration as Peter was forced into a run by the very same girl who had just pushed him.

It took him a moment to see the other people out there, Karl had called out, and now they seemed intent to leave.

That was when things got weird, a deafening sound of thunder filled the hallway, and Karl was suddenly surrounded by crackling electricity.

Victor stood up with the aid of Yuki and looked at the door, the light began to fade and there was a lot of shouting from outside, the pair looked to each other and then back to the door.

Victor narrowed his eyes as he took in what was happening, he seemed to know something more than Yuki as the white haired boy was properly freaking out.

Victor turned to him and placed a hand to his shoulder and smiled.

"Listen Yuki, we need to find Crystal quickly, whatever you do, do not leave my side unless I think it's safe."

This seemed to calm Yuki down a bit, but not enough to form words. At that moment Karl opened the door and looked at him.

For all intents he seemed like a different person, his features were sharp but the most noticeable change was the fading red colour in his eyes.

"You both need to go to the dance hall, quickly"

Victor nodded and gripped Yuki's arm, but instead of heading to the hall he swung around the back of the school. A group of men in black suits ran by him and he frowned while looking at them.

"Yuki, this is serious, we cannot afford to be seen by those men, not while we are unsure as to who they are after. I believe it might be Peter, but till we can be sure, we are not safe?"

It didn't seem to make sense to Yuki, but right now he just wanted to do as he was told.

"I am going to find Crystal, don't move from here okay?" Victor said this to Yuki who nodded at him, and then he left.

He made his way to the main hall again, dodging out of the line of three more agents that ran past him.

He made it to the hall just in time to see one of the agents gripping to Crystals arm, it was clear the man was about to take her but he was not about to let that happen.

A ring of blue flames shot up around Crystal, forcing the man back away from her, and Victor gripped him by the shoulder and spun him to face him.

"Touch her again and you're dead. Understand me?"

The man furrowed his brow and made to pull out his gun, this just caused Victor to sigh and next thing the man was on the ground with a glazed look in his eyes.

The flames went down to reveal a terrified Crystal, she looked to the man on the ground and then to Victor and as he expected, she screamed and made to run away, it was a short chase for him to catch her, and a shorter struggle with him holding her to his chest.

"Calm down Crystal, I need you to trust me till we can get somewhere safe"

Her heart was thumping against her chest and she shook her head, but he held her by her shoulders and looked her into her eyes

"Brigid, we are not safe"

Crystal's eyes widened as a voice replied in her head. 'You need to listen to him' and instead of helping her to calm down, it freaked her out more.

But Victor didn't have the time to calm her down properly as Simon rounded the corner and ran towards him.

"Victor, they have Peter and they know who you are, one of the others saw the flames."

Simon said as he came to a stop in front of the taller boy

"They are sending agents to your house, I contacted your parents and they are evacuating as we speak, but you are not safe."

Simon was holding Megan, she seemed lifeless under his arm and Victor looked to her for a moment and then back to Crystal

"We can't stay here, but my house is not safe, can we go to your home?"

She looked at the girl and then to Simon before she nodded in agreement, Victor smiled and took Megan from Simon.

"Thank you Crystal. Simon, can you go get Yuki and find us after? Make sure neither group follow you"

Victor said as he turned to Crystal once more.

"We need to hurry, I can't hold this displacement spell for much longer"

--

As they ran towards the gates Crystal began to understand what Victor meant about a displacement spell.

Even though they were in plain sight, no one seemed to actually see them. They made it out of the school and booked it down towards her house without anyone noticing as a result.

Claire opened to door in a panicked state and gripped Crystal into a tight hug.

"Oh hunny, I was so scared. It's all over the news that something is happening at your School"

She pulled her back and looked to Victor and the girl he was holding

"Quickly come in."

Victor stepped in and placed Megan to the couch, she was hardly breathing and there was terrible black bruising all around the area she had been darted in.

He ripped open her top and wiped away some of the puss coming from her wounds with the scrap of fabric he got from said top, Claire came in with a first aid kit but Victor just shook his head.

"That won't help her, we need Eir"

Claire frowned and really looked at Victor then, it was clear that there was more to this boy that she had let into her home, and she looked back to her niece before she asked Victor.

"Just who are you?" She said, and Victor smiled just before Crystal answered.

"He is a friend from School aunty, he saved me, his name is-"

"Hades."

Victor stood and faced Claire.

"My vessel is Victor, but what you are asking is who resides in me. And the answer to that is Hades. Brigid resides in Crystal. And I have found two more like us. One of them is on their way. That is Eir."

Just as he said that a knock came to the door, Crystal looked at it but didn't move. It was only after another knock came that Victor moved to answer it.

Simon walked in with Yuki in tow, he was covered in blood and just as Victor was about to close the door, a whine halted him.

Outside was a huge wolf-dog, and in its mouth was a boy, Thomas to be exact.

Victor moved to the dog and took the boy from its mouth, he was pretty badly bloodied, but not in danger of dying, the dog visibly shrunk in size till it looked like a small wolf, and it followed Simon into the house and finally Victor entered and closed the door.

"Crystal, could you make some tea. I think this is going to be a long night for us"

He smiled at her and she laughed, not the 'haha that's funny laugh', but more the 'I am too far gone to even know what to think anymore laugh'

She shook her head and left the room to put the kettle on, and Victor moved over to Yuki.

"I am going to need your help, but I want you to trust me on this okay?" Yuki nodded and moved closer to Megan as Victor gestured to her.

"Okay, give me your hand"

Victor took his hand and stabbed one of his fingers with a scissors from the first aid box. Yuki yelped but didn't pull back, and Victor repeated the motion on his own hand, once done he placed the two cuts together.

A pulsing energy flooded between them, and Victor who was clearly in pain from it spoke through gritted teeth.

"You need to wake up, we need your help to save this girl."

Yuki opened his eyes and turned his head slowly to look at Megan

"Why should I save her?"

His voice was distorted, but Victor smiled, it was working.

"Because she can help us find Peter. Or as you know him Eir. Loki."

Thank you for reading.

Please feel free to follow me on instagram under
the user name
'Genesisgoboom'

Or follow my Facebook page
www.facebook.com/craftylikeafox